His smile was unpleasant as he explained

"My secretary had an imagination that would have done credit to a romantic novelist. She decided to fall in love—with me. It did not make for efficiency."

Lora felt very sorry for her predecessor. "It happens," she said tartly. "It's unfortunate, but where you get impressionable people, you get regrettable attachments."

He was watching her, the hooded gaze as penetrating as a shard of yellow diamond. "But not you, Miss Reynolds."

She looked back at him, lifting her rounded brows in a movement she'd found extremely effective in the past. "Not me, Mr. Duncan."

Their eyes met, held—almost, she thought dazedly, clung. It was terrifying. Yet it was exhilarating, because her strength matched his, her guard held.

ROBYN DONALD lives in northern New Zealand with her husband and children. They love the outdoors and particularly enjoy sailing and stargazing on warm nights. Robyn doesn't remember being taught to read, but rates reading as one of her greatest pleasures, if not a vice. She finds writing intensely rewarding and is continually surprised by the way her characters develop independent lives of their own.

Books by Robyn Donald

Don't miss any of our special offers. Write to us at the following address for information on our newest releases.

Harlequin Reader Service
P.O. Box 1397, Buffalo, NY 14240
Canadian address: P.O. Box 603,
Fort Erie, Ont. L2A 5X3

ROBYN DONALD

a matter of will

Harlequin Books

TORONTO • NEW YORK • LONDON
AMSTERDAM • PARIS • SYDNEY • HAMBURG
STOCKHOLM • ATHENS • TOKYO • MILAN

Harlequin Presents first edition March 1991
ISBN 0-373-11343-9

Original hardcover edition published in 1989
by Mills & Boon Limited

A MATTER OF WILL

CHAPTER ONE

'YOU look as though you've had a rough night.' Gavin Browning's voice was acid.

He was her superior, but Lora's expression didn't change. 'Blame Yoosy Jasper.' Her tone invested the name with scorn.

The habit of privacy was too deeply ingrained for her to say more, but the sour look in Gavin's eyes was replaced by a taunting envy. 'And what's the world-famous rock star been doing to you? Did all that money and fame, not to mention the widely touted sex appeal, act like a blowtorch on the ice you drape yourself in?'

Lora had pale blue eyes, clear and cold as crystal, rendered compelling by the dark density of the lashes that surrounded them. She let them survey the man behind the desk with a total lack of expression. 'He thinks,' she said evenly, 'that temporary secretaries are up for grabs. Literally.' And, as Gavin's hot brown survey fell to the smooth swell of her breasts, she added, 'And your last comment comes fairly close to sexual harassment. Sheila wouldn't like that.'

He flushed, as she had known he would, and there was a distinct tinge of uneasiness in his reply. 'Hell, you blasted feminists have no sense of humour. There's no need to go running to the boss just because I make a normal masculine comment now and then. I can't help it if a pretty girl pleases me.'

Lora said scornfully, 'Pretty? I'm not pretty. And I'm a woman, not a girl. What have you got for me? Sheila said it involved travelling.'

Sheila was the owner and manager of an organisation that specialised in providing the right person for any temporary position. Lora's brother had been working for her for five years when he had introduced his sister. To her intense surprise, because she was only four years out of high school, after a gruelling interview she had been accepted.

That was two years ago. In the interim Sandy had left New Zealand for Canada, but Lora still enjoyed the life, one which made use of all her skills. Since the beginning of that year she had acted as hostess at a dinner party for Members of Parliament held by a visiting millionaire, typed the manuscript of an award-winning novel while the writer's regular secretary had her baby, and travelled to India with an industrialist because his personal assistant had broken her leg climbing a mountain.

Much of the work was difficult, some of it highly confidential. As well as being absolutely trustworthy, Lora was good at her job, and she knew it, and so did the man who watched her from behind the desk.

He smiled unpleasantly. 'It seems that one of our biggest landowners needs someone totally reliable to get him out of the mess his latest secretary has left behind. I'd have sent Barbara, only she's gone and got herself the flu, and Jim is in Hong Kong. Besides, he wants this paragon to help him organise a large function for a group of buyers from Asia and South America. With your language skills, that means you are the logical choice.' He gave Lora a malicious smile. 'It's Matt Duncan.'

Lora could tell that it pleased him to watch her lose her formidable control. For a moment the blood drummed in her ears, but she bit on to her full lower lip and took a deep breath before saying evenly, 'He won't let me on to the place.'

'He won't know who you are. You and Sandy are only half-brother and sister, you don't share the same surname. You do look alike—at least Sheila says you do, I can't see it myself—but your colouring is different.' He permitted himself another sly smile, watching her from beneath his lashes as the pale skin over the striking framework of her face tightened then relaxed.

Satisfied, he resumed, 'If he's a normal man, and from all the rumours he's very normal, he won't get beyond your—er—*striking* physical characteristics. He likes pretty girls. After all, Amber Stephanides lived with him for nine years, and she's a beauty.'

He smiled again, unpleasantly, and let his eyes wander over her face. A spark of something flared in the depths of his eyes. He said harshly, 'So, of course, are you, although you do your damned best to dress it down. A proper ice maiden, all coldly classical good looks without a hint of warmth to you. I admire Yoosy Jasper for having the courage to try to get you into bed, even if he was too stupid to see that you'd freeze him to death if he got you anywhere near him. I imagine Matt Duncan's ladies have to work quite hard for their pretty trinkets; cold Nordic beauties are probably not his line, unless the man's a masochist. The Stephanides woman is a redhead, if I remember correctly. All fire and passion.'

Lora looked her contempt as she got to her feet. He had been careful not to say that Amber Stephanides had been Matt Duncan's mistress, but that was what he thought. Not for the first time she wondered what made Sheila keep him on as an executive, and not for the first time reminded herself that she was the only one who seemed to rub him raw. Most of the other workers liked him.

'When do I start?'

'Tomorrow.' He waited until she was almost out of the door before saying, 'I might see you up there.' Watching with satisfaction as her head whipped around, he concluded smugly, 'I get my holidays in a few weeks. I've always wanted to see the Bay of Islands. If I ring you up, Lora, would you go out with me?'

'No.' Her voice was unemotional, but she didn't like the sound of his laughter as she closed the door. However, she didn't waste time thinking any more about him. Apart from his position as her immediate superior, Gavin Browning had no place in her life.

However, his comments about Amber Stephanides stayed in her mind. While she packed that night she found herself thinking of the woman. Married when they were both little more than children to Alex Stephanides, one of the richest men in the world, she had had left him for nine years to live with Matt Duncan. There was some blood tie between them, but gossip had been vigorously insistent on a different sort of relationship. Lora stood with a pale green dress hanging loosely in her hands and recalled the features of the billionaire's wife, so vivid that even newspaper photographs couldn't dim the impact of such beauty. For a moment her features hardened; then she lifted her wide shoulders in a shrug and continued her deft, efficient packing.

Sheila had called her in to her office a few minutes after she had left Gavin Browning and been much more conciliatory.

Tapping the letter on her desk with a long forefinger, she had said, 'I like it as little as you do, Lora, but I honestly don't see what else we can do. We nearly lost him over your brother's affair. We can't afford to say that we can't supply.'

'Would it be so drastic to lose the great Matt Duncan's favour?' Lora couldn't hide the corrosive undertone to in her voice.

'Yes,' Sheila said simply. She sent Lora a not unsympathetic look, but her expression revealed that she would not be moved. 'Not only does he use our services, but he knows or went to school with everyone who has any influence in New Zealand. Over the years he's put a lot of business our way. You've been here long enough to know how it works, Lora. Our ability to deliver and our reputation for discretion mean everything. Sandy talked, and that's why he was fired.'

Lora nodded. 'Yes, I know.' In spite of herself, she could not hide the bitter inflection she gave to the words.

The older woman gave an infinitesimal shrug. 'It was a hard lesson for him to learn.'

She didn't mention that she had fought to keep Sandy. Not that her efforts had been to any avail: Matt Duncan had been implacable. Neither did Lora say anything about the excellent reference Sheila had written for her brother when at last he had been forced to leave the country.

Now Sheila said slowly, 'I've always thought that there was more to the affair than any of them ever admitted. Has Sandy ever indicated——?'

'No, we don't talk about it.'

'I must say I've never come across anyone who is as incredibly reticent as you two. It's a real asset on the job; a pity Sandy let a pretty face coax him into forgetting it.' Lora tensed, but Sheila went on briskly, 'I'm rather sticking my neck out sending you up there, so try not to let the man know who you are, will you? Not that I want you to lie. Matt Duncan doesn't like liars, so if anyone sees any resemblance and taxes you with it, for heaven's sake admit it. You and Sandy have the same bone-structure—and identical eyes, same colour, same shape, and those lashes! Only your hair is much fairer, the authentic ash-blonde. Scandinavian heritage?'

'Our mother's ancestors,' Lora told her, 'came from the Faroe Islands, I believe.'

Sheila nodded, all businesswoman again. 'And keep yourself to yourself—we don't want a repetition of poor Sandy's experience.'

'Don't worry,' Lora said acidly. 'I wouldn't have Matt Duncan if he were delivered to me on a plate. With an apple in his mouth and a bottle of the very best French champagne.'

Sheila smiled, although her eyes were watchful. 'Just remember that. He's an absolutely gorgeous creature, all six feet plus of him. Quite lethal.'

Lora lifted her brows at her. 'Oh?' The syllable expressed a total lack of interest.

'Really. A lion of a man, gold and tawny, with that lazy arrogance that intimidates us lesser mortals.

However, he's also as tough as old boots, and very, very astute, so try not to allow your natural dislike of him to show. I imagine he's more accustomed to women falling at his feet than repelling him with that infuriating blank stare you've made peculiarly your own. And although your loyalty to Sandy does you credit, remember that Matt Duncan had every right to demand that we sack him.'

Lora got to her feet. 'Yes, I know.' She gave Sheila a small smile. 'I won't let him know that I think he's a vindictive bastard.'

Sheila frowned. 'No, I wouldn't do that. He doesn't strike me as a man who would take that sort of attitude from anyone. He has that enviable, arrogant confidence of someone who has always had his own way.'

It was on the tip of Lora's tongue to mention Amber Stephanides, who had left Matt to go back to her husband, but she didn't. Sheila did not approve of gossip, and in spite of all the fascinated speculation no one really knew what had happened in that interesting triangle.

And she, she reminded herself, was not in the least interested. She would help Matt Duncan to the best of her ability, and then she would come back and forget him. It would be a simple exercise in will-power.

Before she had left the room Sheila asked, 'Have you ever been to the Bay of Islands?'

Lora shook her head. 'No, although I realise it's almost tantamount to treason to admit it!'

'It's very beautiful, and, even though it's our usual diabolically wet spring, it should be better weather up there.' Sheila looked out of the window at the drizzle and finished wryly, 'Warmer, anyway.'

Lora elected to drive herself up in her own car. On the map it looked like a journey of a couple of hours; she had not taken into account the fact that there was only one main road north, and for much of its length it wound around and through the hills that gave the long northern peninsula its particular character and beauty.

Nor had she anticipated the enormous cattle trucks or the tourist buses, and the fact that those same steep hills were obstacles to such behemoths.

So she was late as she ground up the last pinch behind a slow Road Services bus. But even so she stopped at a little lookout at the very top of the hill and got out, stretching her long legs and back, pushing a hand up to loosen the tight knot of her hair.

It had been a cloudy, still day, cool and damp, with an expectant, springlike feel to it. The clouds had not moved on, but the light had altered so that the indented sheet of water in front of her was the colour of old pewter, reflecting in the hammered grey surface the astonishing green of the hills and islands. Eastwards, out to sea, the declining sun illuminated a bar of gleaming silver stretching from the northern headland of the bay to a lesser promontory on which stood a tiny village that had to be Russell.

Lora drew an enraptured breath as her gaze was drawn downwards by a small vehicular ferry chugging fussily away from a wharf at the bottom of the hill. There were islands, small and romantic, and tree-covered headlands, and a white-sailed yacht slipping silently through the water towards a safe haven in the bay below.

Lora's too-controlled expression relaxed into sheer delight. The air was fragrant with salt and the balsam of manuka. She leaned against the car and closed her eyes, listening to the rapidly diminishing groan of the bus as it disappeared through tall trees towards the bottom of the hill. From somewhere down the steep bush-clad slopes to her right a blackbird sang, sweet and shrill. Ahead was Matt Duncan. But at this moment was peace.

Sighing, Lora anchored a tress of hair into the bun at the back of her head and reached into the car for the map. As with everything the agency did, it was efficiently marked with the location of the station. Past the village of Paihia and through a golf course, then a short run alongside a forest of pine trees, and she would be there. The station was close to the sea; Lora frowned as she looked for the homestead, only slightly disappointed when she saw that it wasn't actually on the coast as so many of the original homesteads were.

Still, there seemed to be several good beaches on the property. The water would still be too cold to swim in yet, but if she was lucky she might be able to sunbathe, and fortify her pale skin with as much of a tan as it ever achieved.

Her eyes shadowed, she refolded the map into its original creases and lowered her long body back into the car. She had never been one to put off an evil hour.

Paihia was busy, a tourist town, but the road past the next two bays was almost deserted. She had to avoid a large chartered coach as she passed the Treaty House car park, but from then on there was little traffic, although quite a few people still played golf on the course. Past the pine forest, dark and silent, along another narrow, dusty stretch of road, and there were two big pillars of volcanic rock with a sign on one and a cattle-grid between.

Lora stopped. The sign said simply 'Kahurangi', which meant, she knew, blue skies. And, whether it was some sort of omen or not, at the very moment she put the car into gear the pall of grey cloud split to reveal the soft, brilliant blue of the sky. A beam of gold arrowed down, radiant, almost tangible, lingering for a few seconds on a clump of totara trees to light up the jade tips of the new leaves. And from overhead came the ecstatic outpourings of a skylark.

Lora drew a deep breath, her full mouth relaxing from severity into a rare, slow smile. She looked suddenly much younger, as young as the adolescent she had never really been. Still smiling, she drove through the tall pillars with no gates, and down a long drive.

There was a crossroads. For some reason this amused her. One arrow pointed to 'Cottages', one to 'Workshop', another to 'Woolshed' and the last to 'Homestead'. Ignoring the aloof regard of several enormous red bulls in the adjacent paddock, she turned the nose of the car towards 'Homestead'.

Around a curve in the drive, a terracotta-tiled roof peeped between a tangle of branches which resolved themselves into two enormous jacaranda trees, one close to the house, the other across the lawn. The house itself was a big double-storeyed place painted white, with grounds of a couple of acres or so about it. It did not shriek of money, but the size and excellent condition of the building and the beautifully manicured expanse of the gardens were evidence enough that Matt Duncan was a very rich man.

Conscious of an alarming hollowness in her stomach, Lora drove in through another pair of pillars, smaller than the ones at the road but still separated by a cattle-grid, and on up the gravel drive, stopping under an elegant *porte-cochère* which protected the front door.

As she turned the engine off, the door opened; she swallowed hard. This was the man who had had her brother blacklisted, hunting him mercilessly until he had to leave the country. She had the feeling that she was going to have to keep reminding herself of his vindictiveness, because the man who came towards her was, to put it bluntly, quite the most exciting man she had ever seen.

She climbed stiffly out of the car, mollified in spite of herself when he kept his eyes fixed firmly on her face. Cursed with a voluptuous body, she hated it when men looked her over as though they expected her to follow through on the lush promise of full breasts and a narrow waist, and the curving, feminine line of buttocks and thigh.

'Miss Reynolds.' It wasn't a question, just a statement of fact in a deep, pleasant voice. 'How do you do? I'm Matt Duncan. I hope you had a good trip up.'

He held out a hand and she put hers in it.

'Yes, I'm Lora Reynolds,' she said inanely. It was un-believable, but she was seized by a distinct shock of re-cognition. She *knew* the unyielding planes and angles of his face, the fine, tawny texture of his skin, the way his hair was coloured in various shades of gold and amber. She recognised the secret fire of topaz in his eyes—lion eyes, cool and dominant, yet almost lazy, a layer of in-dolence overlaying the hidden strength. She knew his smile, the warmth of it, the slightly cynical twist at the corner of the finely moulded lips which made it obvious that she was staring.

The whole situation was rapidly taking on a surreal-istic atmosphere. Hastily she pulled her hand free and turned back to the car.

'I'll bring your luggage in,' he said, amusement and something else colouring the deep, calm voice.

She didn't want him to handle her battered old suitcase, but there was no way she could say that. Help-lessly she unlocked the boot and waited while he lifted the case from it, trying to recover her usual frosty com-posure, the poise that had been so hard-won and which had never let her down until then. It was an effort to keep her eyes from his tall figure, clad in a fine cotton shirt tucked into narrow-fitting trousers that smoothed down over long, heavily muscled legs.

His voice was somewhat surprised as he hefted the case in one strong hand. 'That's all?'

'That's all.' Lora picked up her bag and followed him through the panelled door into a wide hall with an ex-quisite flight of stairs leading up to the first floor.

'Your bedroom is upstairs,' he said. 'On the left.'

She went lithely up in front of him, stopping when he indicated a door; the room had wide windows and looked out on to the sea through the bare, sleek branches of the jacaranda.

'I hope you find it comfortable,' he said as he put the suitcase on to the bed. He straightened and turned, catching Lora's helpless gaze on the ripple of muscle across his shoulders.

Something flared into the golden eyes, at once hardening and intensifying the brilliant colour, but to Lora's relief it faded immediately, subdued by an implacable will. He said crisply, 'Come down when you're ready, and I'll show you around the house and give you something to drink.'

The breath which had been trapped in her dry throat eased out in a long, silent sigh as he closed the door behind him. Danger dazzled her with warning signs. She would have to be very careful not to let him see again the heady compound of attraction and dislike which held her in thrall. It shouldn't be too difficult, she decided sombrely as she swiftly unpacked her suitcase. She was accustomed to controlling her emotions.

After a quick shower in the tiny but extremely opulent bathroom, she changed into a neat dress that did its best to tone down the blatantly feminine contours of her body, and combed her hair, pulling it fiercely back into its knot at the base of her neck. It was not particularly flattering, and that was the way she wanted it to be.

Allowing herself one despairing query—Why this man?—she walked out of her pretty bedroom and, with caution very much to the fore, went on down the staircase, admiring as she did so the beautifully carved native birds and foliage that sprang up and intertwined to form the banisters.

'The original homestead was a monstrous Victorian edifice on the beach.' He must have hearing like a cat's, because she had made no noise coming down the carpeted stairs. Startled, Lora looked up. He was standing in a doorway a few paces along the hall, his expression enigmatic as he watched her. He was so tall that even two steps up she was only just his height. And in perfect proportion—but her mind clamped down its censor and she managed to concentrate on what he was saying.

'It burnt down early in the century and this was built to take its place, but by some whim of the flames the staircase was barely touched and my great-grandmother insisted it be incorporated in this house. Purists object to its Victorian ornateness.'

'Do you?'

He managed to look arrogant and amused at the same time. 'No, possibly because I grew up here—it's always been just part of the house. Come and have something to wash the dust from your throat.'

He took her into a large room. Apart from the book-shelves on the walls, it was a far cry from the pleasant smoking-room atmosphere the designer probably wanted to achieve. This was a working office, complete with cupboards and filing cabinets, a large executive desk and a smaller one at an angle with a computer console on it. But it had a fireplace with a fire burning cheerfully in the grate, and in front were two armchairs and a table.

'Sit down,' he said, gesturing to one of the chairs.

Lora had only just lowered herself when a woman came in carrying the tray. She was middle-aged and pleasantly rounded, with rather sharp eyes. Her name was Mrs Crawford and she was the housekeeper.

It was deceptively pleasant sitting in front of the fire and pouring tea for Matt Duncan; deceptive because, although he acted with the easy confidence of a good host, Lora knew that those hard eyes were watching her every movement, assessing, appraising, formulating decisions on the basis of his impressions. Cursing that moment of awareness upstairs, she understood that he had recognised it for what it was, and he was making sure that she got the right idea.

Which was: thanks, but no, thanks. Strictly business, that was how Matt Duncan saw her, and that was how he wanted her to see him. She wouldn't have been human if she hadn't been a little piqued by his tactful but very definite rejection of anything personal between them, except that she agreed wholeheartedly with him. Sandy's experience was engraved on her mind.

It was dangerous to get involved with this man.

Dangerous in many ways, ways she didn't need to consider because he recognised the peril just as she did, and he was making sure everything stayed very much under restraint.

Pushing her thoughts firmly to the back of her mind, she listened as he spoke of the work he had for her. She asked questions, intelligent questions. His answers pulled her brows together and she said tentatively, 'I had no idea that things got out of control so quickly in a business like this...'

'They don't,' he replied grimly.

She was taken aback, then relaxed, assuming that his last secretary had been incompetent, which surprised her as he looked the sort who would sniff out incompetence at a hundred yards.

He smiled, rather unpleasantly, and explained, 'My secretary had an imagination which would have done credit to a romantic novelist. She decided to fall in love—with me. It did not make for efficiency.'

Lora felt very sorry for her predecessor. 'It happens,' she said tartly. 'It's unfortunate, but where you get impressionable people, you get regrettable attachments.'

He was watching her, the hooded gaze as penetrating as a shard of yellow diamond. 'But not you, Miss Reynolds.'

Very definitely she looked at him, lifting her rounded brows in a movement she had found extremely effective in the past. 'Not me, Mr Duncan.' A wry, sardonic note overlaid the soft clarity of her voice.

Their eyes met, held—almost, she thought dazedly, clung. It took all her resolution to withstand that merciless scrutiny. A strange chill feathered across her nerves; she felt that he was trying to pierce through her protective barriers, to penetrate right into the shrouded depths of her soul. It was terrifying—yet exhilarating, because her strength matched his, her guard held.

And with the right amount of conviction. She saw satisfaction warm that cold appraisal; mixed with the approval was a hint of purely male speculation which should have made her a little uneasy. But at that moment she was a little arrogant in her relief, pale eyes gleaming beneath dark lashes as she smiled with just a hint of complacency, full mouth curved in a smile which came too near to smugness.

It vanished when he asked abruptly, 'How old are you?'

'Twenty-three.'

He nodded, but the appraisal remained in his glance. 'You look younger.'

'I can assure you I'm competent,' she began stiffly, surprised because most people took her to be older than her years.

He interrupted with a charming, slightly mocking smile. 'Oh, I'm sure you are. The agency is noted for its efficiency, which is why I use it, and on the rare occasions that it falls down, it makes amends as quickly as possible.'

Sandy, she thought bitterly.

He resumed, 'I have no fears for your efficiency. It must be your hair that makes you look young. That incredible flaxen shade is rarely seen in anyone past their teens.'

A prickle of antagonism ran up her spine at the lazy, almost insolent note in the deep voice. Smiling dismissively, she said in her sweetest tones, 'Surely not, Mr Duncan? It's astounding what can be done with dye and bleach nowadays. Almost every starlet has hair this colour. And any other she needs.'

He lifted his brows in a movement which had probably intimidated quite a few people in the past. It did cause Lora a swift tension, but she refused to be impressed. 'After all,' she pointed out reasonably, 'you have most unusually coloured hair. Sort of marmalade, isn't it? Very pretty...'

He laughed, obviously enjoying her wide-eyed imitation of artlessness. 'I prefer to think of it as just missing red,' he said, 'and I get the message. I promise not to comment on any of your other physical attributes.'

He seemed to mean it, too, which was a relief. Lora hadn't missed the purely masculine way his eyes had surveyed her most obvious female features. He had not been blatant or obnoxious about it, but there had been no doubt that he was all male in his appreciation.

Briskly she began to ask him questions about the station, trying to fit together the snippets of knowledge she already possessed so that she would be able to work independently as much as possible.

'What I need most is complete updating of the files,' he said. 'Have you used one of these computers before?' At her nod he went on, all business now, 'I'm afraid you'll find a real mess. I had to take over while the manager of the beef stud recovered from an operation, so everything is behind. I'll be able to work with you for the next couple of days, but after that I have to go to Auckland and you'll be on your own for possibly a week.'

Lora liked the sound of his voice, clear and cool and incisive as he went on to tell her exactly what he wanted her to do; he was completely conversant with all that went on throughout his holdings, apparently. As well as this office, he had one in Auckland, run by an accountant who dealt with the ramifications of what was obviously a great pastoral and agricultural conglomerate.

After a few minutes he looked at her absorbed face and said abruptly, 'I didn't mean to start you off immediately; you must be tired. I thought you might like to go over the station now with me so that you get some idea of the place, then we'll begin work properly tomorrow morning. How does that sound?'

For the first time she was able to relax with him, giving the slow, sweet, open smile which came so rarely. Only later did she think that it was, perhaps, a strange reaction to a man she had every reason to hate.

He seemed taken aback at her response; his eyes narrowed so that she looked hastily away, but once they were in the Land Rover and travelling over the smooth, well-kept gravel roads of the station that momentary stiffness evaporated. Lora had worked for agricultural concerns before, so her comments were intelligent and knowledgeable.

'You are obviously familiar with agricultural operations,' he observed. 'Have you specialised in this branch of your work, or did you grow up on a farm?'

The shutters came down over her face, leaving it rigid with composure. 'Yes,' she said, hurrying immediately into some query about the logistics of running a place like Kahurangi as a series of studs, rather than as one holding devoted to beef and sheep.

'Because it's more profitable,' he said calmly, after a slanting, speculative glance which worried her.

She said in a desperately level voice, 'But that wouldn't apply to every situation, would it? I mean, Kahurangi is much bigger than the average New Zealand farm, even bigger than most stations except the high-country ones in the South Island.'

'It is, and no, this sort of concern wouldn't be possible everywhere, but most agriculturalists have seen the writing on the wall and are diversifying as much as they can.' He nodded towards a herd of red deer behind high netting fences. 'Once over the fluctuations that are inevitable for any new industry, deer should become an excellent export. They have less fat in the meat than beef and lamb, and the by-products are guaranteed a sale in Asia.'

The corners of Lora's mouth tucked in as she recalled photographs she had seen of deer antlers sawn and stacked in piles for the Eastern market.

Rightly interpreting her involuntary shudder, he said coolly, 'Sentiment doesn't enter into the cold, hard world of balance-of-payments deficits, Lora.'

'Didn't I read something about researchers discovering that mutton is lower in cholesterol than was believed?' she asked.

He sounded a little startled. 'Yes. Scientists of the Meat Industry Research Institute have tested New Zealand meat, and discovered that, with all visible fat removed, both lamb and mutton are lower in saturated fatty acids than chicken.'

The Land Rover had been climbing slowly away from the homestead towards a set of stockyards; as if hit by an idea, Matt turned off the road through a gate and took the vehicle up a steep hillside and out on to a level, grassy spot. Here he switched the engine off and turning to Lora, watching her as he continued, 'As well, our animals are all grass-fed, so the meat has no residues, no hormones and is free from industrial pollution.'

Made cautious by his regard, she stirred but matched him valiantly. 'Aha, but what about the dreaded cholesterol?'

'Well, it seems to be generally accepted that the cholesterol content of the food we eat is not particularly important in avoiding heart disease. Saturated fats are the villains. So if all visible fat is cut off so is most of the danger, especially as half the fat in lamb is poly-unsaturated. Moderation,' he finished blandly, 'seems to be the key.'

Lora looked out of the window at a view her eyes didn't see. Her vision was filled with an image of a man who had never been moderate in his life. Her father. A tiny shudder pulled icily at her skin. In a toneless voice, barely audible, she said, 'Yes. Isn't it to everything? The only way to live?'

'It's surprising to find someone of twenty-three espousing such a restrained, temperate policy.'

She looked blindly across at him, forcing a smile in an attempt to match his ease. 'Is it?' she said finally. 'But life can become so untidy if one indulges in violent reactions.' The cold chill cleared. She saw him watching her with half-closed eyes, and didn't need to look hard to see that he was thinking, finding out more than he should from her involuntary response.

A muscle tightened beside her mouth. She said aloofly, 'I have a father who enjoys extravagant emotions. I found I got tired of it after a while.'

There, that should put him off. It was almost the literal truth, but she had managed to phrase it so that it became the amusing trait of a man in love with drama, rather than the bitter, terrifying aberration that had made the lives of all her family a living hell until those who could had fled as far away as possible and rarely went back.

She thought fancifully that the clear gold of Matt's gaze was like a torch, burning through all the barriers she had set up, outlining her features with fire. It was ridiculous to be so aware of this man, ridiculous and dangerous... Her mind raced, thoughts tumbling over themselves in an unsorted turmoil, coloured by nameless emotions, and then he moved, turning away from her so that she saw only the clear-cut nobility of his profile strongly silhouetted against the blue of the sky.

And, while she was pondering the reason for tagging him with such an unfashionable adjective as 'noble', he said slowly, 'So you believe in safety first?'

She darted him a suspicious little glance. Surely he wasn't the sort of man who saw challenges in even the most innocent observations, and felt they owed it to some macho image they had of themselves to respond?

But that little glance reassured her. He was smiling, his tawny eyes limpid and amused as if he'd read her thoughts.

'Definitely,' she said fervently.

His laughter rang with an oddly comforting note. 'So,' he said with smooth confidence, 'do I. If you look to your right you can see a clump of eucalypts on top of a hill—yes, over there. Behind and below them is Kerikeri. Have you ever been there?'

'No. No, not yet. I've seen photos, of course, of the citrus and kiwi-fruit orchards, and the Stone Store that the early missionaries built.'

'The oldest building in New Zealand is there too, the original mission house. You'll like Kerikeri. It has charm and a certain style. But the whole of the bay is interesting.'

'And beautiful,' she said quietly, looking around just as one of the dogs on the back of the vehicle leaned over and uttered an impatient bark into the window, as if to demand the reason they were still in the cab.

Matt's chuckle joined hers. 'He's right, I brought you up here to give you some idea of the lie of the land. Hop out.'

They were not on the highest point of Kahurangi, but well above much of the surrounding countryside so that the land fell away beneath them in sweeps of green and gold until it reached the border of the sea. In this light, with the pall of cloud which had hung over her all the way up from Auckland now banished by a south-westerly wind, the colours of land and sea were bright and vivid, bold as spring.

Jolted by pure pleasure out of her habitual reserve, Lora said as much, and he smiled with a certain proud satisfaction, then laughed as he caught her peeping at him from beneath her lashes.

'All right, I do feel a proprietorial and quite undeserved personal interest in the landscape. I was born here, and I hope to die here.' He turned his head, nodding at a group of graves half hidden under a huge pine tree. 'My father and mother and my grandparents are buried there. I enjoy people's pleasure when they see the bay for the first time.'

'I think I understand.' Her voice was flat because she was trying to hide the envy. How would it feel to know exactly your place in the scheme of things? No wonder he had that bone-deep confidence that seemed to border on arrogance. Matt Duncan was almost literally monarch of all he surveyed, and he enjoyed and valued his place in the world, whereas her father's attitude had almost managed to convince her that she had no right to be born, no reason to be alive.

Because she was afraid of those perceptive eyes, she turned away from him to study the scene below, from the manicured slopes and valleys of Kahurangi to the hills to the south where the blue of the bush was occasionally broken by splashes of white clematis, spring's harbinger.

Hanging over the water of the quite substantial river that ran beside a road were kowhai trees, golden with blossom, graceful as a Chinese print. Another splash of white had her squinting.

'Is that a waterfall?' she asked delightedly.

'Yes. The bank you can see covered in trees is the end of an old lava flow, and the waterfall is where a small creek has hollowed out a passage over it and down to the river. It looks low from here, but the cliff is over a hundred feet high and the waterfall is dangerous.'

'It looks beautiful,' she said.

He smiled. 'Beauty is always dangerous.'

For some reason she thought of Amber Stephanides. Turning away to hide her expression, she asked, 'Where was the volcano?'

'There are no obvious vents, but the original landscape all around this area and north beyond Kerikeri was covered by great basalt flows. The little volcanoes dotted around came later.'

He pointed out several of them, most with the faint terraces that marked sculpturing by the ancient Maori for use as forts, or fighting *pa*. Lora didn't have to feign her interest; like all enthusiasts, he swept her along with him so that she thought she understood some of his affection for this land he held as a trust.

'It's like being one of the gods in Olympus,' she observed, watching a flock of sheep being moved from the yards along the race towards a paddock. The sound of their plaintive bleating drifted up through the crisp air, intermingled with the authoritative barking of the dogs and the shrill imperatives of the shepherd's whistle.

'Unfortunately.'

Something in his voice alerted her; following his frowning regard, she watched with concern as further along the track a man on horseback put his mount at a fence, clearly seeking a short-cut back to the homestead complex. Lora held her breath as the horse faltered and then crashed through the wires, throwing its rider on to the ground where he lay ominously still.

Matt said one word, a savage expletive, then turned and strode back to the Land Rover. He didn't appear to be moving very fast, but so rapid was his long-legged gait that Lora had to run to keep up with him.

CHAPTER TWO

THE ride back down the hill and across the paddocks lived afterwards in Lora's mind as the most frightening time she had ever spent in a vehicle.

Although she realised almost immediately that Matt Duncan was a superb driver, totally in control, the speed at which they were travelling and the bumps and hollows in the ground threw her about like a shuttlecock, so that she had to cling to the seat-belt to keep upright.

And when he set the Land Rover over a bank far too steep for anything with wheels, she couldn't prevent a frightened gasp that only terminated when they made it to a more level piece of ground.

Wondering grimly how the dogs were faring in the back, she risked a glance over her shoulder. They were balancing themselves without much difficulty, tongues hanging out in a fashion which could only be described as eager.

She ran her first-aid training through her brain again, hoping with a fervent hope that when they got there it would be to find the unlucky rider on his feet and lacking any obvious signs of injury.

Not so. He was very still on the ground, lying on his back with his arms outstretched like a discarded doll. Lora looked at Matt as he switched off the Land Rover's engine and got out. Beyond a slight pallor, there was nothing to reveal any emotion. His decisive features were rigidly disciplined as he strode across to the man on the ground.

Lora hurried to join him, dropping to her knees on the opposite side of the still figure.

Matt said clearly, 'Tim! Can you hear me, Tim?'

Muscles beneath the skin of the young male face moved slightly, as though the urgency of the demand was getting through, but it wasn't until Matt said forcefully, 'Damn you, Tim, answer me!' that there was any response. After a stretched second, Tim turned his face towards the stony profile of the man beside him.

Lora's hands were moving gently over the long limbs, searching for broken bones, when he said fretfully, 'Matt... Dis-dislocated my damn shoulder, Matt...'

'I'll dislocate your damn head! You know better than to put a slug like Blossom over a fence! No, don't try to answer me!' He looked across at Lora, who was running an obviously competent hand down Tim's leg. 'Anything?'

'No.' She stood up. 'Nothing that I can find, anyway, but I don't think we should move him until a doctor's seen him. I'll stay while you go and get help.'

'I'll use the radio in the Land Rover,' he said briefly, getting to his feet.

Lora sank down again, looking with compassion at the man on the ground. Even bruised he was very handsome, his face long and aquiline, with a humorous twist to the mouth that his dazed state hadn't banished. He seemed very young and vulnerable.

A sudden frown corrugated the unlined brow and she put her hand there, saying quietly, 'It's all right, you're going to be all right. Don't worry.'

Behind them Matt's voice had finished snapping out crisp instructions. One of the dogs came across and gave a polite sniff in Tim's direction before sitting down not too far away, the sharp, intelligent eyes fixed on his pallid face.

Tim's frown deepened. He groaned, slowly opening his eyes to fix Lora with a startling blue gaze. 'Wow,' he said succinctly, then winced.

His pupils, she noted, were the same size, a good sign. Smiling at him, she said, 'Your shoulder is going to hurt until it's replaced, I'm afraid. Lie still. Mr Duncan's organised help and you're going to be all right.'

He said earnestly, 'Lady, I've got a headache like nothing I've ever had before. Don't take your hand away, it feels good there. What's your name?'

'Her name is Miss Reynolds. Can you stop flirting for long enough to tell us where else you hurt?' Matt's voice was brusque.

Startled by his abruptness, Lora sent him an admonitory glance over her shoulder, and was shaken to find herself subjected to an arrogant warning glare. The hand on Tim's forehead stilled, then was withdrawn.

Tim said muzzily, 'Everywhere. Except where you were stroking.'

'Tim!' It was the tone of a man rapidly losing patience.

It might have been totally unsympathetic, but it got results. Tim opened his eyes again, to fix Lora with a resigned look which held lurking humour.

Lora smiled with great sympathy and he said, with more exuberance than he had a right to feel, 'You've got a lovely smile, Miss Reynolds. It's just my shoulder, Matt, I promise you. I can feel all the rest of me and it feels OK. Bruised, but normal. Except my pride, of course. I don't think that will ever recover.'

'Oh, you'll overcome that.' Matt's retort was dry, but Lora heard the note of relief and liked him for it.

A burst of garbled talk from the radio in the Land Rover summoned him back to the vehicle.

Tim muttered, 'Don't go.'

'No, I won't go.'

'Matt...' he said, slurring the word. 'I'm sorry...'

'Shh, don't talk.'

Lora saw him shiver and took off her jacket, draping it around his shoulders as well as she could. When Matt came back she was holding Tim's hand and talking softly to him, soothing platitudes which seemed to ease his discomfort. Without a word Matt stripped off his heavy woollen jacket and arranged it over the long legs.

'How long will the doctor be?' she asked.

'Not too long.'

Lora said with relief, 'Good.'

'You seem very competent.'

She didn't like the way he was watching her. It made her distinctly wary, but she replied in a calm tone, 'I've done a first-aid course, as obviously you have too.'

'There are enough ways for an accident to happen here to make it necessary for everyone to have some grounding in first aid. I insist on all my workers doing the St John course.'

She nodded, and he dropped down beside Tim and touched the back of his hand to his forehead. Nothing altered in his expression, but she saw him look back towards the homestead, and knew that he was concerned. And indeed, Tim seemed to get paler by the second.

Tensely, she sat in the grass with Tim's hand clutching hers until at last Matt said, 'Ah, here she is now.'

Sure enough, a car was bumping its way towards them, followed by a grey and white ambulance. And after them came two men, one on a horse, the other riding a farm bike with two dogs balanced behind him.

While the doctor checked Tim, Matt coaxed the horse from the tangle of wire in which it was placidly standing as it viewed with benign interest the accident it had caused.

Lora watched covertly. It took him immense patience and a considerable amount of guile to remove the animal from its wire trap, and he seemed unaffected by irritation when it showed its independence by jibbing several times. When it was free, he sent it back to the homestead with the horsemen. It looked a little sheepish, trailing along with its reins held so that its head was turned towards its captor.

Within a very short time the ambulance was easing its way down the track as the doctor, a majestic middle-aged woman, observed cheerfully, 'You can't kill some people. He'll be thankful you keep your tracks as smooth as any road, Matt. How's young Nick Stephanides, by the way?'

'Fine.' Matt grinned. 'As you say, you can't kill some people. Last I heard, he had set up a flying fox from the villa to the beach and is having a wonderful time swishing through the olives fifty times a day.'

The doctor laughed as one who was well accustomed to the vagaries of that particular child, and said professionally, 'Nothing showing up from that bash to the head?'

'No, never. He's fully recovered.'

'How about you? Leg still aching?'

Matt grinned down at her. 'No, not a bit. Now, shouldn't you be attending to young Tim before you give Miss Reynolds here the idea that we spend most of our lives either incurring or recovering from severe injuries?'

The older woman gave him a companionable grin back. 'When you get people who are reckless, you're bound to get broken bones,' she pontificated, and burst out laughing at Matt's suddenly austere countenance. 'Yes, you don't like to think that in your own way you're every bit as rash as young Tim! It's a wise man who knows himself, they say.'

With which parting shot she took herself off, revealing more than a little rashness herself in the way her comfortable Volvo shot off down the track.

Matt said resignedly, 'That's what comes of having a doctor who delivered you. No respect.'

Lora liked the lighter side of him revealed in this conversation, but it didn't last long. By the time they reached the homestead he had become very cool and abstracted.

'Will you tell Jane that I'm going to the hospital? If I'm not going to get back in time for dinner I'll ring her.'

By following her nose, she found her way into the kitchen and found Jane Crawford putting the kettle on for tea as she talked to a very pretty Maori woman with a little girl on her hip. After Lora had passed on the message, Jane introduced Meri Sutton. 'And Moana,' she added, flicking a loose black ringlet back from the mischievous little face. 'Meri's husband Rod is manager of the beef stud.'

Meri grinned. 'For his sins, he's directly responsible for Tim, so he'll get a rocket from Matt when he comes back.'

'That Tim Catchpole is a tearaway and a show-off,' Jane said severely, 'and I wouldn't be surprised if he manages to kill himself one day!'

'Not, I hope, while Rod's his boss.' Meri's voice was so comically prayerful that both other women laughed, as Meri said teasingly, 'I'm glad you like him too, Jane. He's just loaded with charm, isn't he, even if he is a bit of a hard case? Just as well his parents are friends of Matt's, otherwise young Mr Catchpole would have been given the order of the boot within a fortnight of getting here.'

Jane firmly cut off a choke of laughter. 'When he decided we needed some gingering up with our Guy Fawkes bonfire?'

By now, Meri was chuckling. 'Oh, yes! It was so funny, Lora. He was in the Territorials and somehow—no one dared ask how—he'd got some explosives——'

'Thunderflashes,' Jane interpolated.

'—and he flung them on the fire. Well, you should have seen—and heard—it! Remember the hoo-hah? All Paihia thought the enemy were landing, and I believe they even heard it over at Kerikeri. The horses went berserk, and the cattle went through three fences, and for days afterwards the hens only laid soft-shelled eggs. Poor old Tim just stood there gawping and said, "I didn't realise they'd make so much noise!" And Matt was furious!'

Both women sobered. Apparently Matt's fury was awesome enough to project itself over time and space. Jane poured the tea and said idly, 'Just as well the

Catchpoles are very friendly with Matt. Even so, I think his father had to do some hard talking. Matt's not a man who puts up with stupidity.'

Was that a warning? And, if so, was it friendly or not? Lora had noticed that the housekeeper was not exactly forthcoming; her attitude seemed to be coloured by faint suspicion. Perhaps she was possessive. Lora had read somewhere that old retainers were sometimes jealous of their place. But Jane was hardly old. Pleasantly middle-aged, she looked far too sensible to go in for that sort of Gothic behaviour. And she didn't exactly fit into the concept of a 'retainer', either.

'Oh, Matt's tough, but he's got a kind heart.' Meri was quite definite about it. 'I know he expects the most from everyone who works for him, but he's just as hard on himself, and Rod says there's no one he'd rather go to if he ever ended up in trouble. And Rod says the reason he gave Tim another chance was that Matt was a real daredevil when he was younger. He remembers what it was like.'

'He was,' Jane agreed drily. 'Reckless as a young stallion; he just about turned his poor mother grey, but he never did anything stupid. He always knew his own capabilities. And he's grown out of it now.'

Recalling that headlong dash down the hill, Lora wondered whether the housekeeper was right, or whether she was trying to convince herself!

'He sounds a perfect paragon,' she said lightly, thinking of the less attractive side of that demand for excellence, the implacable harrying of a man who had let the great Matt Duncan down.

Jane bristled. 'There aren't many men who deserve the sort of loyalty Matt expects, and gets. He's a natural leader.'

And a natural despot, Lora thought defiantly. However, she was wise enough to keep all signs of such rebellion from her manner and face. She knew hero-worship when she heard it; Jane would probably find excuses if Matt Duncan robbed a convent!

After all, her mother had found excuses for her father—she was still doing it, regardless of the fact that he had driven both her children from home and terrorised her into ineffectuality.

In spite of Lora's caution, however, she sensed that Jane was not going to make up her mind about her until she knew her better. A woman who had built her own adult life on wariness, Lora could appreciate the housekeeper's attitude, so it was surprising that she felt a little stab of hurt.

Not enough to drive her from the room, however. It was pleasant to sit in the large modern kitchen and drink tea and watch Moana play contentedly with a peg and the small milk saucepan clearly kept for her own special use, but too soon Meri saw the time and gave a squeak of alarm.

'I'll have to go home and put the dinner on,' she said, hastily getting up. 'Come on, Moana, time to go, lovey. Rod will be in soon, and if I know anything about his methods of childminding, both he and Pete will be filthy!'

Pete, Lora already knew, was Meri's three-year old son, already as good a rider, his doting mother said, as anyone on the station. 'And from the way this one always wants to go and see the horses, she's going to be as horse-mad as he is!'

Moana looked up alertly, saying, 'Horsies?' as she scrambled to her feet.

When they had left, a silence fell in the kitchen. Lora broke it by offering to help wash up, and was politely but definitely rebuffed.

'No, that's what the dishwasher's for. If you have something else to do, I'll begin on dinner.' Jane gave her a small smile. 'I work best alone.'

Well, that was plain enough. Lora returned the smile, but turned away before she saw the surprise in the older woman's face, and said, 'I'll unpack properly, then. What time is dinner?'

'Matt eats at eight, but he usually has a drink in the parlour at half-past seven.'

Lora was struck by a thought. A little uncertainly, she said, 'I suppose—perhaps he'd rather I ate in the kitchen.'

This brought her an old-fashioned look. 'This is New Zealand. While you live in the house, you eat with Matt. And anyone else who has been asked to dinner.'

That was plain enough, too. Lora went thoughtfully up to the bedroom, stopping just inside the door to look around the gracefully harmonious room with pleasure. It was a lovely mixture of the sophisticated, as typified by an elaborate lacquered dressing-table that was clearly old and valuable, and the country style, with the use of a pretty, fresh chintz for the bedcover and the curtains. The ceiling and woodwork were painted the same cream as the background to the chintz, the walls a warm primrose-yellow. An old kauri campaign chest served as another dressing-table, the brassbound corners polished to a mellow glow. There were flowers, brilliant cobalt irises in a modern crystal vase, and late jonquils and violets, the mingled scents very fresh and sweet.

Lora thought that she would have liked whoever had done the decorating. Although 'decorated' seemed too formal a description for a room that looked as though it had grown organically. She wondered whether Matt Duncan's bedroom was the same mixture of modernity and English-country-house styling, and was startled to find heat crawl across her skin as an image of him bending over a bed flashed across her mind. Those wide shoulders would block out the room...

It was, she told herself, striving for her usual objectivity, merely because the man was so handsome. But Tim was even more handsome, his features more conventionally attractive, yet she had no forbidden images of him to banish.

Tim, of course, was young.

Twenty-five or twenty-six, her mind reminded her with relentless logic. Older than you.

She refused to continue this ridiculous train of thought past the realisation that Tim seemed young to her because she had always been old, had never known what it was like to be carefree.

Lora was good at banishing things she didn't want to face; she had had a lot of practice at it. Activity helped, so when she had finished unpacking and stored the case up on the shelf in the built-in wardrobe she went in to the en suite bathroom and ran herself a bath.

Made thrifty by her stoical realisation that she was unlikely ever to be able to trust a man enough to marry him, she had been squirrelling away a good proportion of her salary ever since she had started work. More than anything else she wanted her own home, and at the rate she was going she would soon have the deposit for a house if she didn't set her sights too high. Her refusal to spend money on the impulse-buying of clothes and cosmetics was another barrier between her and most women of her age; they didn't understand her passion for security.

So to lie in a bath and use the exclusive and delicious toiletries she found in an elegant little cupboard gave her a frisson of pleasure, sybaritic and secret, an upwelling of sensual joy from the hidden deeps of her personality that normally she would have ignored, even despised.

Later, flushed, her hair clinging in damp tendrils to her skin, she pulled the plug and climbed out, drying herself briskly and with impersonal speed, so accustomed to long legs and skin like silk that she thought nothing of them.

She did, however, spend some time pondering about her choice of clothes. Over the years she had built up a wardrobe, discreet in cut and colour, suitable for any occasion including a formal ball, and she prided herself on never looking out of place wherever she was. Tonight, she decided, was no time for anything too formal, yet this house and Matt Duncan did not exactly suggest a casual outfit.

She pulled out a silky dress, sleek and smooth, eyed it thoughtfully and put it back with a tiny sigh. Not a sensible buy; it was too sensual, the material fluid over her breasts and hips. Instead she chose a cream polyester crêpe shirt with a V-neck and long sleeves over a slim skirt of the same colour, separating them with a wide belt several shades deeper. With it she wore small gold ear-rings and a gold bracelet, and shoes the same colour as the belt.

Just right, she decided, staring at herself in the mirror. Neat, attractive, yet with the faintest hint of businesslike efficiency and a total lack of sexuality. She was not in the habit of gazing at her reflection, but for a few seconds she lingered, wondering how she appeared to others—to, say, a man.

She knew that her full bust appealed to a certain sort; she frowned as her eyes roved over the curves of breast and hips. What made a woman attractive to a man? What was the basis of this unknown pull between the sexes? What was it about, say, Matt, which drew every feminine eye, when Tim, classically good-looking, had nothing of the same charisma?

Her hand touched her waist, moved to cover her heart, and the fingers folded into a fist. Matt was a lion of a man, a heartbreaker, with a potent sexuality which was more than the glowing virility of his appearance. The forceful lines of jaw and chin, the lazy appreciation of his smile, the lithe economy of movement and the hinted-at strength of the lean, muscular body—all these attributes were important, but it was their combination with an effortless authority which demanded respect that made him the sort of man who was exceptional.

Lora's mouth set into a hard, straight line. Angrily she turned away from the mirror. Yes, exceptionally rich, exceptionally powerful and totally unscrupulous in his use of that power. And she was an idiot to let any man, however sexy, set her mooning in front of a mirror.

Cursed with a passion for punctuality, she was ready well before time. She filled in the minutes by standing at her window, watching unseeingly as lights looped together to make a thin, fragile chain around the shores of the bay. Nagging at the back of her mind was the expression on Matt's face as he had watched her beside Tim. It had been fretting her ever since she looked up to see it; something had made him withdraw from the easy companion he had been up on the hill. Afterwards, he had been so cool. Had he somehow made the connection between his new secretary and Sandy? Perhaps she had done something, made some gesture, tilted her head in such a way that he saw Sandy in her.

Her first impulse was to tell him, to admit the relationship. She hated living a lie. She would have risked telling any other person.

Any other man but Matt Duncan, who had already proved by his behaviour that he was vindictive...

A resurgence of the hatred she had felt for him tasted bitter in her mouth, clouding her normally clear brain. It would do no harm to remember that he had driven Sandy out of the country. She hated him because he was powerful, because...

Because, she admitted sadly, he was all the things she hated in her father.

And that, though perhaps understandable, was dangerous. Her father was sick; other men were not like him. Her mind knew that, but it was a little difficult to convince the frightened child inside her.

Her comprehension of the basis for her feelings was not helping her to work out what she should do in this situation. In the end, some two minutes before she was due to go down, she decided to wait and see how he behaved, take her cue from him. If he taxed her with her resemblance to Sandy, she would admit the connection and see what his reaction was.

He was waiting for her in the parlour, standing as she had been at the window and looking out; she wondered whether he too was wondering what to do. He hadn't heard her come in, so she was able to look her fill of him, her eyes roaming across the wide stretch of shoulders beneath the fine cotton shirt.

She had made no movement—indeed, she was sure the breath had stilled in her throat—but he sensed her presence and swung around, those strange golden eyes sharp as crystals.

'Good evening,' he said, the words formal, the tone cool.

Lora felt like a child caught with the chocolate wrapper in its hands. Hastily she asked, 'How is Tim?'

This did not ease matters. His brows drew together. 'As well as can be expected. He's conscious, and keeps asking for the Valkyrie.'

Lora's face remained blank, but some of her response must have showed because he gave a soft, mocking laugh. 'Not your most favourite nickname, I gather.'

'I hate it.' And that was astonishing too, because ever since she had realised that her protests made teasing even more pointed she had refused to admit to anyone just how much she despised it. This man had the power to tip her off balance.

He smiled rather ironically. 'Yes, you're very conscious of your dignity, aren't you? And the Valkyries were not exactly dignified. But you must admit that if you could hit a high "C" there's not an opera house in the world that wouldn't give you a part as Brünnhilde.'

Poker-faced, she shrugged. 'Or you as Siegfried.'

He laughed, and the potent charm leapt into life. '*Touché*. Now, can I get you a drink? Sherry?'

'Yes, thank you.' She was grateful for the prosaic demands of courtesy. As he poured the sherry she managed to pull her composure tight and seamless around her like a cloak. It helped, but several times during the half-hour that followed she had to remind herself that this man had probably been just as affable, just as courteous a host to Sandy the night he had arrived at Kahurangi.

Dinner was served not in the enormous room dominated by a splendid table big enough to seat at least twenty, but in a smaller family dining-room, and in spite of her words Jane did not eat with them.

The meal was superb, chilled pea soup followed by fresh asparagus, with delicious beef, and after that there were strawberries from the garden, eaten with cream.

'Jane's husband is the general handyman,' Matt told her. 'Fortunately for us all, he's as dedicated a gardener as his wife is a cook. Compliment him and he'll be your friend for life. However, don't offer to help him weed. He's learned through bitter experience that most people don't know a radish from a thistle.'

Lora's chuckle sharpened his amused regard. 'I don't myself, so I'll confine myself to compliments.'

'More wine?' He had poured a full-bodied Chardonnay with dinner, and a little still lingered in the bottom of the bottle.

'No, thank you.' She enjoyed wine, but too much made her restless. And she mistrusted the little twist at the corner of his beautifully moulded mouth. To drag the conversation back on to safer ground, she said, 'Can you tell me exactly what you need me to do while I'm here?'

'Come and sit in the parlour while we talk,' he suggested.

The parlour was big enough to take in all of her flat, but it was comfortably furnished in an eclectic style with one or two pieces of excellent modern furniture and a superb antique secretaire on one wall. French windows opened out on to a terrace, hidden now by long curtains which Matt pulled aside so that he could look out into the night. His hair gleamed amber in the light of the lamps as he turned his head.

'Come and see,' he said.

Lora went obediently across, and there on the horizon was the moon, enormous and copper, faintly threatening in its power and beauty as it rose above the edge of the sea.

'It's beautiful,' she said on a soft sigh, then, 'No, that's not the right word. Awe-inspiring. So far away, and yet it sets the tides in motion and affects us—the whole world—in ways science still doesn't fully understand.'

'Yes. It's no wonder it figures so largely in legend and worship.'

He wasn't looking at the moon over the sea, he was looking down into her face; and in his own, in the depths of his eyes, there was a slow, predatory burning, so that the urbane gentleman who had looked after her comfort all evening was gone. In his place, through his eyes, another, more primitive male looked.

And what he saw, he liked.

Lora felt a strange leap of her pulses, a response to that basic pull between the sexes, and froze. Very slowly, as though too swift a movement would loose the barbarian she recognised, she pulled away from danger.

A small muscle worked in her throat. She couldn't wrench her gaze from his, but she managed to say in a voice that had only the merest tremor in it, 'You were going to tell me about my work, I think.'

His hand on the curtain relaxed, letting the folds of material fall free. They moved a little restlessly before settling into the perfect pleats of the decorator's art. It was like coming back to safety and civilisation after being shown a glimpse of wild chaos, beautiful yet dangerous in its lack of control.

And, if Lora felt a stab of sorrow at turning her back on what he had offered, she had the strength of mind not to show it.

Which was just as well, for his expression was cool, any emotion hidden beneath a mask of control. Lora didn't know whether he had been testing her, tempting her to see whether she would succumb to his golden attraction as his previous secretary had done, or whether for a few moments he too had been enchanted by a moon-spell.

Jane broke the tension when she arrived with coffee; after a quick discussion with Matt about some people who were coming for dinner the next evening, she said goodnight and left them. When she had gone, he asked Lora if she would pour, and told her that he liked his with a small amount of cream, just as she did, which gave her strange and very suspect little glow, and increased her wariness tenfold. As she performed the humdrum little task, she wondered if perhaps with this man the hitherto dormant needs of her own heart and body were going to be more treacherous than his virile masculinity.

Over coffee, he told her what her duties were. 'First of all, to clear up the mess that my last secretary left behind,' he said shortly. 'Between the two of us we should be able to get things in some sort of order. Then I'll need your help with a field day that we're having here for a group of agricultural officials from Asia and South America. They have a tight schedule and can only be here for twenty-four hours, so we decided that a field day was the best way to show them what we are doing.'

'Will there be just animals from Kahurangi, or from the district?'

He frowned. 'From all around Northland. I think we were chosen to host it because we have such a selection of animals neatly contained in the one place, and because we are close to hotels, but we don't cater for everything! Pigs, for example.'

Lora's eyes widened. 'Pigs?'

'Many people in both continents rely on pig meat for their protein. We may have breeds or methods of rearing them that will help improve the national stud.'

She drank more coffee and said, 'I see. At least, I can see where all the organising comes in.'

'Yes. Foreign Affairs. The Ministry of Agriculture and Fisheries. And of Trade. And an assortment of others.'

'It sounds like a very high-powered lot of people you're going to entertain.'

He didn't seem at all perturbed. 'It is. And you're going to entertain them too, as my hostess at a party I'm giving the night before.'

Lora's mouth opened, then shut. She said crisply, 'I know that you expected me to play some part in looking after them, but hostess? Are you sure?'

'Yes. You come with the highest of recommendations from the agency, and you speak Japanese and can make yourself understood in Spanish and Malay, which are important. And as you'll be doing all of the organising, who could be more suitable?'

'A mother?' She looked across at him. He was leaning back into his chair, the light of a lamp sending waves of tawny fire through his hair as he moved his head to look at her, a smile somehow hardening his mouth.

'No mother.'

'Well, someone you know—a woman friend?'

He smiled sardonically, as though he had been waiting for her to say that. 'No girlfriend at the moment. Don't you think you can do it, Lora?'

She took a grip on herself. It had been years since she had allowed herself to be intimidated by any job she was given, but her natural competence seemed to have deserted her.

Or perhaps it was some instinct rooted in the obscure past, which warned her that by working for any length of time for Matt Duncan she was walking into danger.

'Yes,' she returned stiffly. 'Yes, I can do it. I have acted as hostess before.'

'I know. Your superior said that you were the best.' He spoke matter-of-factly, as though of course he wanted—and got—the best. It successfully quenched her astonishment at Gavin's praise.

Then he asked, 'And what about you? Is there a boy-friend or lover waiting for you to get back to Auckland?'

Afterwards she never knew whether it was an inborn instinct which encouraged her to say, 'I don't think that's any business of yours, Mr Duncan. I promise you I'll do my best to make sure this field day goes off perfectly for you.'

Amusement gleamed in his smile, but his voice was as cool as hers as he replied, 'I'm sure you will. I have every trust in you. Do you think you could bring yourself to call me by my first name? We're very informal here, and if you go on calling me Mr Duncan in that admonitory way, everyone might think it's because I need to be kept in my place.'

Ruthlessly suppressing an answering sparkle of humour, Lora said repressively, 'Of course.'

'Then say it,' he commanded.

She actually had to pronounce it carefully, and even then her mouth behaved as though it didn't want to taste the word.

But when she had got it out, sly mockery glinted beneath his lowered lids and he said smoothly, 'There, that wasn't so bad, was it?'

Lora fumed with unvoiced resentment. However, there was one way to stop him making fun of her, so she got to her feet, looking down at him from her loftiest angle as she said, 'I think I feel a little tired. Do you mind if I go up to my room?'

He, too, rose in one loose-limbed movement, and she lost the ascendancy. There was a streak of dulcet humour in his voice as he returned, 'No, of course not. I'll see you tomorrow morning.' He waited until she was almost at the door, her backbone so straight that she felt the strain, before saying blandly, 'Breakfast is served in the morning-room, which is next to the kitchen, as soon after seven as Jane can get it on the table.'

'Thank you. Goodnight.'

It was no parting shot, but it was the best she could think of; she was not, however, surprised to hear his low chuckle as she stalked out of the room.

CHAPTER THREE

LORA awoke the next morning clear-headed and calmly ready to begin work. Some time during the night her subconscious had convinced her that that unnerving incident in the light of the wakening moon had been no more than his way of testing her. It was distasteful, even humiliating, but she already knew that he was a ruthless man. And, to be fair, his experience with his last secretary would make any man wary.

She even allowed herself to be rather pleased that she had passed his trial by moonlight. After all, the moon was known to have interesting and aphrodisiac qualities. Not to mention the well-known fact that lunatics were named after it!

A small smile hovered on her mouth as she came down the lovely, elaborate staircase and followed her nose to the breakfast-room. She felt ready to deal with anything.

The sun poured in a crisp golden flood through french doors and across the wide, dark boards up to a table laid for two. On a sideboard there were mutton chops and bacon and toast, stewed tomatoes the colour of garnets, and four muffins carefully enclosed in a linen napkin. Coffee sent its delicious scent before it, mingling pleasantly with the clove perfume of the bunch of pinks in the centre of the table.

The room was empty, but almost before she had time to become aware of it Matt came in, clad in dark blue trousers and a cotton shirt which barely hid the sleek muscles of his torso beneath fine pale blue material.

Something peculiar happened in the region of Lora's stomach as she replied to his smile and his greeting. Nothing, however, disturbed the smooth serenity of her expression. She ignored the way the sun gleamed like thick honey over his smoothly combed head; she ignored the sudden singing in her nerves, the prickly tension in her skin when his hand brushed accidentally across hers as he passed her the butter.

She was physically attracted to him, and that was as far as it was going to go. She was not going to allow herself to weave fantasies about this man, of all men.

So she sat opposite him in the joyous ambience of the spring morning, cool and fresh in her green shirtwaister dress, neat and groomed and remote, and smiled and ate although both felt as if they were choking her, and forced to the furthest recesses of her mind the astounding, shameful betrayal of her flesh. Self-discipline had become a vital part of her character, cold and tough and glossy like an opaque film over the warmth deep in her heart's core. One of the first lessons she had learned in her childhood was that it was dangerous to reveal that soft inner part of herself. It left her vulnerable, open to all sorts of abuse and manipulation.

It had taken years, but she had learned well. Now no one got beneath her shining coat of self-sufficiency. She was not afraid that Matt would discover that the sight of him made the blood quicken through her body.

Afterwards she went up and made the bed and tidied the room, then, at nine o'clock exactly, knocked on the office door. He called for her to enter, standing with automatic courtesy as she came in; one glance at the pile of papers on the desk showed that he must have been at work since early in the morning, possibly before dawn.

'We keep regular office hours,' he said, noting the direction of her glance, 'but there are occasions when I need to work longer. Now, the first thing for you to do is get the files into order. Heaven knows what system your predecessor used, but I've been unable to make head or tail of it. See if you can.'

She couldn't. Filing was a job she hated, but after a while she began enjoying the puzzle, working away at it with something akin to the pleasure of the hunt and the satisfaction she felt when she solved a clue in a cryptic crossword.

Matt worked hard, occasionally breaking off to dictate answers to the papers he was reading, so that it was a shock to both of them when Jane brought in a tray of tea and shortbread.

'Ah, that looks delicious. We'll have it out on the veranda, thank you.' Matt lifted his head and smiled, and Lora could see why Jane was so protective. There was affection in that smile, and a warmth that had not yet been directed towards her. She refused to accept that the odd coldness in her heart was envy.

Wide, and furnished with comfortable outdoor furniture, the veranda was a perfect place to drink tea and watch the antics of a flock of white-eyes plundering the fruit from a guava bush in the border. Lora's gaze drifted past the tiny green-grey birds and on along the border, pausing with pleasure at azaleas in brilliant glory, a clump of white flag irises, and pink mounds of thyme humming with bees, its fragrance evocative and wholesome in the still warm air.

Further along, an Australian waratah held high its great crimson cones of flowers; she watched eagerly as a tui twisted and turned about one, drinking the nectar from each floweret, the sun gleaming green and brilliant cobalt across his back, highlighting the bobble of white feathers at his throat. In between sips he made contented whirring noises, interspersing them with lovely notes like the chiming of small bells.

'Are you interested in birds?'

She tried to tell herself that Matt's voice was an intrusion, breaking into her wholehearted absorption. She turned her head, the wonder and delight fading to a smooth mask of conventional pleasure in her face. 'Yes,' she said simply. It was too blunt, almost discourteous, so she added, 'And gardens. This is beautiful.'

There was definite pleasure in his eyes as they surveyed the beauty all around. And why not? Lora asked herself waspishly. Anyone who owned all this had every right to be self-satisfied.

'Come with me,' he said, and rose to his feet.

Surprised, she followed him across the lawn towards a tall shrub which had panicles of pink flowers over it. He waited until she was beside him before skilfully and delicately parting the scented veil of flowers so that she could see into the inside of the shrub. A thrush sat as still as a statue on her nest, her head lifted so that her beak pointed skywards, her bright, frightened eye fixed desperately on the intruders.

Lora's slow, wondering smile lit up her face, lingering after he allowed the leathery leaves to mesh together. In accord they waited until they were half-way across the lawn before they spoke, and then it was Lora who broke the silence.

She said quietly, 'Thank you.'

He was frowning a little, his eyes hooded as they skimmed across her face. Instantly her face assumed the expression of guarded watchfulness that she wore as armour. His glance sharpened, but although there was a note of constraint in his tone he said affably enough, 'If you continue working as hard as you have been, I'll show you the nest of a *riroriro*. Have you ever seen one?'

'No.'

'It's one of the miracles of nature. A little pear-shaped pouch suspended from a twig, woven from grass and moss and spiders' webs, with its entrance at the side, a step and a tiny porch over it. It's guyed by ropes to other twigs to keep it steady in the wind.'

She was enchanted, as much by the pleasure in his voice as by the image of the tiny nest. Something warm and peaceful moved in her heart; without thinking, she laughed and said with a swift upward glance, 'I'd love to see one. I promise to work very hard.'

As they came to a halt at the edge of the veranda he looked down at her, dark brows separated by vertical grooves. Lora's heart gave an uneven leap into her throat and his eyes came to rest there for a long, taut moment while the almost mischievous humour faded from her expression.

His eyes returned to hold hers. She thought she saw puzzlement in the tawny depths, and a growing determination, and she was afraid. But his voice was aloof as he said, 'I'm sure that I don't need to bribe you with birds' nests. You can be trusted to do your work properly.'

A pink flake of colour touched each high cheek as pleasure at the compliment made her catch her breath. Danger bells clanged through her brain. 'Thank you,' she said a little stiffly, and for the rest of that day she treated him with a formality that seemed to irritate him into reciprocating it.

The people who came to dinner that night were a neighbouring farmer with his wife and niece, and a couple from America who were staying at the hotel at Waitangi. Lora wore another of her secretary dresses, a tactful swathe of polyester in a muted blue, and was startled to realise that both of the older women wore designer fashions, very elegant and, she would have thought, a little too elaborate for dinner in the country.

Their dresses, however, were nothing compared to that of Keren Smithers, who came with her aunt and uncle. Although it was far too sophisticated for a girl no older than eighteen, Lora was dazzled by the sensual swathe of black silk and lace that set off Keren's black hair and white skin to perfection. She was not, however, as impressed by its wearer.

'Oh, another one,' Keren said on being introduced. Her rather opaque stare ran curiously, dismissively over Lora. Then she turned to Matt, long and lean and elegant in his dark suit, and laughed. 'I was certain you'd get a male secretary after your shattering experience with the last one.' A sideways glance at Lora followed, pointed and malicious. 'The idiotic girl made an immense nuisance of herself mooning over Matt. It was thoroughly embarrassing for everyone.'

'Including the poor secretary,' Lora purred. Apart from solidarity with one of her kind, she had had enough of being warned off. It was not as though she looked anything like a *femme fatale*. Matt Duncan she could understand; he was, after all, paying her not to fall in love with him. But Keren Smithers was nothing more than a pain in the neck, intent upon staking a claim that might, or might not, be valid.

'Still,' she resumed sweetly, 'I suppose one shouldn't be too harsh. Better to be able to fall in love than not. No doubt she'll emerge from the experience of unrequited love a wiser, stronger woman.'

There was an interesting silence. Matt looked amused. Keren Smithers' eyes narrowed. Lora smiled limpidly back down at her, shamelessly making use of her height to intimidate.

After a moment the shorter woman said snidely, 'Let's hope so. Goodness, you're tall, aren't you? And so well-built!'

Lora smiled so hard, her cheeks ached. 'Yes. I'm very lucky.'

Matt broke it up by asking Keren what she would like to drink; Lora didn't know whether the gleam in his eyes was appreciation, or the promise of retribution later.

After that the evening was more enjoyable. Lora took care to stay out of Keren Smithers' way, and tried not to feel irritated by the way the woman hung on Matt's every word. She had to be the most obvious creature in the world. Immature, too. Her conversation consisted entirely of gossip and flirtatious remarks, to which Matt responded with a courtesy that was not quite avuncular. When anything else was discussed, she sat pouting prettily until she could turn the subject.

In spite of herself, Lora was curious to know what Matt thought of Keren's efforts to indicate that there was a relationship between them, but it was impossible to tell. He was an excellent host, urbane and witty, with a gift for directing conversation so that everyone was displayed to advantage, but Lora couldn't rid herself of the feeling that, although he appeared to be enjoying himself, he was in some essential way detached from the whole proceedings.

Afterwards, when he came in from seeing his guests off, she was clearing the glasses away. He said briefly, 'Leave it. Jane will do it in the morning.'

She said, 'My mother always told me to clear up on the night.'

'Your mother,' he countered drily, 'didn't have Jane to deal with.'

When she made no attempt to put the glasses down, he reached out and caught her wrists, preventing any movement with a loose hold. 'Put them down,' he ordered softly.

She went white. Her hands made a strange, convulsive jerk and she stood unbreathing, his size and closeness summoning memories she had thought long repressed.

'What is it?' he asked harshly.

Her tongue came out to dampen her dry lips. Forcing the words past an obstruction in her throat, she whispered, 'Nothing. I—I just don't like being held. By the wrists.'

'I see.' He released her immediately, and stepped back, his amber eyes concerned yet very speculative. 'I'm sorry.'

She said miserably, before she had time to assess whether it was sensible or not, 'It isn't you.'

'I see,' he said again, slowly this time, and she had the unnerving notion that he did indeed understand the years of abuse that had made her supersensitive to any constraints.

She hesitated, wondering if she should explain further, and looked up into a face carved into lines of fierce and implacable domination. A strangled little sound escaped her lips as she cringed away.

She straightened up immediately, but it was too late. Shock, pure and simple, registered in the handsome face, and then was wiped off.

'Go to bed,' he said.

Without a word she put the glasses down and left him. But it was hours before she got to sleep, and when she did it was to dream and mutter restlessly.

She woke with circles under her eyes and an old fear brought ruthlessly to the surface. Make-up got rid of the circles; the fear she had to talk away.

It was ridiculous to be so sensitive about it; after all, she had stopped having nightmares about her father's abuse once she had been able to convince herself that he could no longer harm her. Perhaps that was why she had reacted so badly when Matt had touched her. She was on edge, anyway, afraid by the burgeoning attraction she felt. Perhaps her mind had confused the old abuse with the prospect of losing her hard-won independence.

Because she knew that he would not physically hurt her.

He wasn't at breakfast and didn't come into the office until after she had settled down to type from the dictaphone. When she looked up he nodded, his expression detached.

She was typing furiously, the earplugs of the dictaphone firmly in place, when Jane came in.

'Tim,' she said succinctly. 'They've discharged him, and he wants to know if someone can pick him up.'

Matt nodded. 'I'll be there in twenty minutes.'

Jane said, 'It won't hurt him to wait for an hour or so; Ted can go and get him, he'll be back by then.'

'He's my responsibility.'

Jane nodded and left the room. A moment later the telephone rang again, and was put through to the office. Frowning, Matt took it. Lora erased a mistake and began to concentrate again. A few minutes later she was disturbed from a fairly complicated passage by a light touch on her shoulder. Switching off, she looked up at him.

'That,' he said with restraint, 'was someone from the Ministry of Agriculture and Fisheries, telling me that a car full of officials are on their way here. I want you to go into Kawakawa to pick up Tim. Take the BMW.'

Lora's eyes widened. 'I'd rather not. I'll go in my car.'

He shook his head. 'Tim has long legs. The bigger car will be more comfortable. It's easy enough to drive.'

It made sense, of course, but she didn't want to drive his car. 'I might,' she pointed out carefully, 'be a lousy driver.'

His inscrutable golden eyes dropped from her face to her shoulders, and thence to her strong wrists and long fingers. 'Anyone as deft and skilful as you has excellent depth-perception. You are quick to react,' this with a sardonic smile that left her in no doubt that he was referring to her instant withdrawal from any sort of overture, 'and very efficient. I have no fears for my car.'

Nevertheless she manoeuvred the thing with extreme care along the roads, glad that she didn't have to take it down too many miles of narrow gravel road.

Tim was waiting impatiently outside the neat wooden building of the hospital, his long body lounging against the wall. When he saw who was at the wheel his face lit up and he came eagerly forward.

'The Valkyrie! What's your name, please, so I can put a label to all my fantasies?'

She grimaced as she leaned over to open the passenger door, but told him mildly enough.

'Lora. I like that. It's nice and old-fashioned. Like Tim,' he said, lowering himself into the seat a little awkwardly as he manoeuvred his arm and shoulder in. He grinned at her, blue eyes sparkling with pleasure and open appreciation. 'Is our beloved leader still mad at me?'

It was difficult enough to keep a straight face, but this last impertinent question made her smother a chuckle.

Setting the car in reverse, she concentrated on getting it out of the parking bay before answering. 'I don't know.'

'Oh, it's easy enough to tell. Does he spit tacks whenever my name is mentioned, or is he still being all silent and rigid about the whole affair?'

Lora negotiated a sharp corner half-way down the steep hill. 'He seems to be fairly even-tempered about the situation, but your name hasn't come up much.'

'Oh, dear,' he said, gloom darkening his brow. 'That means that he hasn't forgiven me.' Almost instantly he cheered up. 'Still, at least he didn't contact my parents.'

'How do you know?'

'Because if he had, I'd have had my mother up weeping all over me.'

From his tone of voice he was clearly pleased about this lack of attention. Lora stopped at the intersection to the main road, waited while an enormous cattle truck and trailer swished past, and turned right. Tim watched with a wary eye while she negotiated another inter-section and headed for Paihia, then relaxed.

'You're a good driver,' he remarked.

She smiled. 'You don't need to sound so surprised! Women are much better drivers than men.'

'You sound like a schoolmistress. That depends on what criteria you judge by, surely?'

'I judge by the only practical one,' she returned drily. 'Safety.'

He laughed. 'Tell me, are you always so repressively sensible?'

She said in her serenest tone, 'Yes.'

'Not,' he said irrepressibly, 'with a face like that and hair that colour. There has to be a streak of dizziness in there somewhere. I shall dedicate myself to releasing it.'

Lora never allowed herself to flirt. She only accepted his overtures now because he was in pain, and because in spite of his air of cheerfulness she sensed that he was

not looking forward to seeing Matt again. And because
some feminine instinct told her that Tim was harmless.

'I doubt it,' she said acerbically.

'Aha, a challenge! No man with red blood in his veins
can resist a challenge thrown his way by a beautiful
woman. I am determined to persuade you that deep down
there's a Lorelei Lee in you.'

The idea of her possessing anything in common with
the gold-digging little survivor of *Gentlemen Prefer
Blondes* made her laugh out loud, the sound rich and
full in the luxurious confines of the car.

He turned his head to watch her, his regard warmly
appreciative. She sobered, for she sensed the speculation
behind the light banter and she didn't want to encourage
him. This situation was complicated enough without Tim
deciding she needed loosening up. He was just a little
conceited, and he was fun, but she was there to do a job
and then get out.

Make no ripples, in other words.

She said lightly, 'I don't go in for challenges, and I'll
have you remember that your boss and mine can sack
me if he thinks I'm not doing the job he's paying me
for.'

'Matt's not stuffy!' He parried her derisive look with
an open blue stare. 'No, I mean it. Oh, I know he comes
on hard and heavy, and yes, I'm not looking forward
to the reckoning for this latest bit of stupidity, but
although he can be pretty ruthless, he's fair. He'll tear
strips off me, and he's got a tongue that could flay a
porcupine, but he's not going to sack me for putting a
horse at a fence! If I'd hurt the animal, that might be
different. Matt's a sucker for the wounded. But he won't
go all Victorian and moral if you and I go out together.
Between you and me, you're no longer allowed to specify
"No Followers" for the domestic help; that sort of thing
went out after the First World War. He doesn't go in
for women in a big way himself—I think because he's

still in love with that cousin—oops, forget I said that! Delete! Wipe the memory banks, please!'

'I don't gossip.'

He sent her a level stare, and relaxed. 'No. You have the sort of integrity that shines in the dark, don't you? I'll bet you've never told a lie in your life.'

If only you knew, she thought wryly.

Recovering his composure with a swiftness that was clearly habitual, he said, 'Well, my mother says that Matt is a closet romantic, and that somehow Amber Stephanides got through his tough, formidable skin, and he fell for her in a big way. Otherwise, why would he be so aloof? Hell, the man can't go out of the door without women drooling over him, but very few get anywhere near him. He won't mind if you and I track around together, provided we both earn our pay.'

'Nevertheless,' she said firmly, 'I'm not going to be here for long, and although I think you could probably charm the birds down from the trees, I'll thank you not to try it with me. Matt may not be stuffy, but I am.'

His grin was completely confident. Although he wasn't looking forward to his interview with Matt, he had all the assurance in the world when it came to women. 'All right, but you won't object if I hang around a bit, will you?'

'Why?'

'You're awfully suspicious,' he complained, for the first time looking a little self-conscious.

'I'm a fast learner.'

He sighed ostentatiously, slanting a swift glance her way. The implacable line of her profile defeated him. 'Oh, well, there's this woman...'

'There always is.'

'She made a big play for me, told me she was in love with me, and then she saw Matt, and she decided overnight that she was in love with him.'

So much for her theories that he had never been refused! Lora felt some sympathy, as clearly it was the first time it had happened to him. Like all men, she thought snidely, his ego probably needed frequent massaging. Although Matt didn't fit that mould. He had the kind of rockbound self-confidence...

Ruthlessly dragging her mind away from its fascination with Matt Duncan, she asked, 'And where do I fit into all this?'

'Well, as a salve to my pride,' he confessed, rueful and endearingly conscious of what he was saying.

His cheek made Lora laugh. 'You should be shot!'

He gave another theatrical sigh. 'Yes, I know, but I could see that you're a good sport. I promise I won't be a nuisance, Lora. I'll just make it obvious that I like you.' His voice hardened and she got a sudden picture of an older Tim, a man to reckon with. 'I'm not in love with Keren, but I think she should be taught a lesson.'

She was tempted, oh, *how* she was tempted, but although Keren Smithers might well be furious if she thought Tim had recovered so quickly, it wasn't likely to stop her from her determined pursuit of Matt.

Anyway, Lora hated deceit. So she said in a repressive voice, 'Possibly, but you're not using me to do it.'

'Oh, all right, be like that,' he said cheerfully. He sent her another glance and said, 'Sorry. But I'm determined to convince you that I'm a perfectly proper man to take you out. I'm mildly amusing and I don't often get drunk and I'm not a sex maniac!'

Lora laughed, and he gave her an immensely satisfied smile and set himself out to be charming for the rest of the way home.

He was not looking so cheerful half an hour later. In fact, when Lora was summoned back into the office it was to encounter a Tim who was pale, with patches of red over his cheekbones and a kind of resigned resentment in eyes that refused to meet hers.

She sent him a sympathetic smile, sorry for his endurance of Matt's bullying, and went back to work. Matt, she noticed, didn't look any different. Apparently he took the intimidation of young men in his stride. Dislike rankled within her. He was, she thought scornfully, a beast, and it would pay to remember that.

He was, however, an efficient beast. She spent the rest of the day with her head down catching up on a pile of correspondence, and as she worked, his crisp voice in her ears, she found a growing respect for him. Compared to some—in fact, compared to any of the other men she had worked for—he was formidably disciplined. Each letter was answered in the fewest number of words commensurate with politeness, in language that was easy to understand even when it dealt with technicalities, as many of them did.

He had wide interests, not all to do with the primary industries. She typed a letter to a big industrialist, and several to various boards and charities in which it was clear he took an active part.

A well-rounded man, she thought a little ironically as she finished a letter setting out a recovery plan for a string quartet based in Auckland which had managed to keep going in spite of horrendous difficulties. From the tenor of the letter it was clear that Matt was prepared to help only because the musicians were helping themselves.

She cast a speculative look at the man who stood by the wall of bookshelves at one end of the room. He was absorbed in some great reference tome, and the severe masculine beauty of his features was emphasised by his complete concentration. He was not, she thought, the sort of man who gave without expecting some sort of return, not necessarily for him but for the community.

The tough angularity of his features, wide brow and long nose, the stark cheekbones stressing the straight mouth, the square blade of his chin—all combined in a symmetry of angles and planes that spoke of a compelling strength and authority. He wore his character in his face. The only hint of softness was around his mouth, and that could have been sensuality rather than any capacity for tenderness.

Lora began to type again, but later that evening, when she was restlessly pacing her darkened bedroom, he invaded her thoughts once more, and she saw his face, his stance, as plainly as if he stood before her. For such a big man he was graceful, although the word sounded too civilised for him. He had the feral litheness of an animal at the peak of condition, each movement smooth and co-ordinated and somehow threatening. Her long hands pushed through her hair, releasing it from its knot so that it sprang, thick and silky and warm, in tendrils around her fingers. She arched her back and neck as the pale flood flowed over her shoulders. An unbidden heat curled through her body, sweet and slow as a tide of honey.

You're pathetic, she scoffed silently, walking across to her window to stare out at the moon rising above the sea. The memory of that strange little interlude when he had shown her its rising came back to her, as it tended to do too often.

As she had too many times before, she relived the enigmatic quality of his approach and her response, the watchful, unstated interest, and the substratum of forbidden emotions that had smouldered beneath the surface.

And not for the first time she wondered if she had been mistaken, if her perceptions had been distorted by all that had gone before. Perhaps this was how her predecessor had felt, spinning fantasies from the mundane conventions of politeness. Matt Duncan possessed an untamed allure that appealed to the primitive in women, so that excitement overrode the constraints of civilisation and the logic of the brain.

The idea was as humiliating as her first conclusion, that she was being tested. All her life Lora had avoided the trap so persuasively baited with the primal instincts. Before she realised that her subconscious was building a refuge for her away from the desires and needs that prompted women to put themselves in the power of those they loved, she had understood that she was never going to marry, never going to fall in love.

And the years that followed had only served to reinforce that decision. She had seen her friends fall in love, watched the erosion of their personalities as they tried to conform to their lovers' expectations.

She had known she could not do it. It would violate some vital part of her character, as rape would violate her body.

But the temptation had never been quite so alluring before. As she stood looking down into the black and silver garden, with the scents of spring, fresh and sweet and potent, rising on the cool air, she thought wearily that life had played a cruel joke, making Matt the one man she could desire.

Or perhaps it was not so cruel. Nothing could come of it; if she was going to indulge herself in an inconvenient passion, then Matt was the safest man to choose.

Suddenly confined by the lovely room, she turned abruptly to the door. It was almost midnight, and she had left Matt only half an hour before and hadn't heard him come up, but she needed to get out into the fresh air enough to risk meeting him on the stairs.

Although a lamp gleamed in a corner of the sitting-room, he was not there; stepping silently, she went out through the french window and along the terrace, stopping only to pick a tiny spray of pink and white jasmine and tuck it in the pale curl of hair behind her ear. The jacarandas were still, boughs held up to the moon. Lora stood for a long moment looking up into the one across the lawn. A small smile tugged at the generous curves of her mouth as she made her way soundlessly across the damp grass. She paused for a moment in the deeper shade beneath the tree, then swung herself up into it and climbed as far as she dared.

Once there she gazed dreamily out across the moonpath, thinking vaguely that it was strange that her fear of heights didn't extend to climbing trees. The jasmine scent drifted, almost too sweet, past her, blending with the fresh fragrance of newly cut grass. She smiled as a hedgehog snuffled importantly across the lawn, feeling a strange kinship with all the creatures of the night.

Kahurangi lay in silver and black beauty spread beneath the ageless, ever-changing patterns of the skies. The tightness in her smoothed out, began to drain away. Lora sighed soundlessly as peace eased the tension in her bones and heart.

Movement in the paddocks beyond the garden jerked her head around, movement that solidified into a horse, and on its back a man. The moonlight gleamed silver on hair that the sun gilded amber. He was riding bareback, although the horse was bridled, and he seemed to be wearing only a pair of swimming briefs. Man and horse, at one in the glamorous haze, the charmed, mystical magic that was moonlight, cantered lightly across grass gleaming with dew.

Lora's breath hurt in her lungs. Her hand frozen on to the branch, she watched as the centaur, the man-horse, pounded in primitive rhythm over the paddocks and down towards the sea. It was a look into a savage, enchanted past, a landscape of Greek myth and passion, and even as she watched the horse and its rider gallop along the sand she knew that this was what had sent her out into the night, this hunger, this restless desire.

She leaned her shining head against the bark of the tree and closed her eyes.

Then, moving with none of the lithe ease which had taken her up the tree, she climbed down and walked back into the house.

Much later, she was still awake when she registered the soft, evocative thudding of hoofs, still lying rigid in the bed when at last she heard the small night sounds that denoted Matt's arrival in the house. A board in the passage at the head of the stairs creaked; she swallowed, almost as though he might hear her heart beating and come in to ask why she had watched him.

At last she went off to sleep, but her dreams were haunted by centaurs, and satyrs, and gods, all wearing the face of the man who had ridden across the landscape of her dreams. And all of them were permeated by the scent of the jasmine she had tucked under her pillow.

There were other dreams, too, dreams she refused to accept or face, pushing them to the back of her mind. In the manner of dreams, the memory faded quickly, so she was able to face him with something like her normal poise over the breakfast-table, although her heart behaved crazily and all through her body she felt the peculiar drawing sensation that she was beginning to recognise as desire.

Clad in denim and a checked shirt, he certainly didn't look like the other half of a creature from Greek mythology, not until she happened to catch his eyes and saw in the brilliant depths a kind of wildness she had not recognised before. Looking hastily away, Lora drank coffee and ate toast as sedately as usual. Until then she had thought that the danger implicit in Matt was that of character, a cold and controlled integrity that demanded the same from those who worked for him, and the will to impose vengeance on those who betrayed him.

After that glimpse of a different Matt the night before, she began to understand that the peril he represented to her was of another sort, not based on reason and logic, but a threat that bypassed the civilised restraints and homed directly in on to her secret core of passion. And that sort of danger frightened her as the other never had, because she recognised instinctively that against it she had no defence.

He would recognise it too, the power of his masculinity over her feminine weakness, and he would know that she was vulnerable to him, that she could be had.

He had said little since he'd greeted her, but now his voice interrupted her reverie, smooth yet with a steely undertone.

'Do you make a habit of climbing trees in the moonlight?'

CHAPTER FOUR

LORA managed to prevent the heated embarrassment in her cheeks from reaching her eyes, but it took all of her strength to face him down so that nothing but cool amusement showed in her expression.

'No, not a habit. It was an impulse.'

'Strange, I'd have sworn that you were a woman who made a point of snubbing impulses.'

That stung, but she shrugged it off. 'Normally I do, but last night was too beautiful to spend in bed. And climbing trees is one of my few accomplishments. I was better at it than my brother.'

And could have kicked herself.

He smiled, his eyes amused as they searched her averted face. 'I preferred cliffs, myself. No?'

For she had given a little shudder. 'No,' she agreed slowly, thinking that if she had any sense she'd not say another word. But something persuaded her into revealing, 'I'm not very good with heights.'

He didn't seem scornful of her weakness, merely nodded as he looked thoughtfully at her. 'Like all phobias, I suppose it's not amenable to logic and reason.'

She understood why his staff liked him so. Firmly repressing an almost intolerable urge to relax her guard, she said calmly, 'Not in the least.'

'But climbing trees doesn't panic you?'

'No. Funny, isn't it?'

'Not necessarily,' he said slowly, pouring out a cup of coffee for her. 'You have some support, and something between you and the ground. You looked very much at home. I saw your hair, like moonlight on the water.' He seemed almost as astonished as she was at the caressing note which wound through the words like a vein of silk. The skin tightened over the framework of his face and a muscle flicked once, twice in his jaw.

There was an instant of strained silence before he continued evenly, 'Do you ride?'

He was making conversation, smoothing over the moment when he had forgotten that he was speaking to his temporary secretary. Lora followed his example; to her astonishment and dismay, she had to first subdue a treacherous flicker of delight called forth by the compliment. 'No, but I admire anyone who rides as well as you do.'

He shrugged. 'I was on a horse before I could walk. If you want to, I can put you up on Blossom.' The amusement expanded into open humour. 'As you saw from Tim's efforts, she's about as safe as your average sofa.'

He was indecently attractive like this. If she refused this offer, one he probably made to every woman who visited Kahurangi, young or old, he might wonder why. The last thing she wanted to do was reveal just how edgy he made her.

So she allowed herself to smile and say lightly, 'I'm not going to be here for very long, so it hardly seems worth it, does it?'

'As you wish.' Clearly she had made the right decision. His face was devoid of expression, but he was probably quite pleased that he didn't have to go through the motions. He held out his cup for a refill and finished, 'I don't expect you to work day and night, you know. You will have time off.'

She nodded, concentrating on pouring coffee without being affected by the lean strength of the tanned fingers holding the saucer. 'I thought I might have a look around the North,' she said. 'I've never been up this far.'

'No?' He didn't try to hide his surprise. 'There's a lot to see, of course, even in the Bay of Islands. If you want to have a closer look at the bay, I'd suggest one of the Cream Trips run by Fullers, who have been sailing around the bay for almost a hundred years, so they know it well. If history interests you, we have much of the early European history right here and in Kerikeri and Waimate North. And there are excellent walks in the forest parks.'

'I want to see the kauri trees at Waipoua Forest.'

'Tane Mahuta and his brothers? Yes, you'll have to visit them. You can't really say you've appreciated the North if you haven't seen the lords of the forest. There is a stand of kauri inland from Kerikeri, but they're nowhere near as big. Tane Mahuta is over on the other coast, a whole day's trip if you want to take a look around the Hokianga harbour.' He drank his coffee and set the cup back on the saucer, smiling at her with immense charm. 'Let me know where you want to go and I'll see what I can organise.'

'I wouldn't dream of asking——'

He lifted a brow, his face settling into an expression that she recognised, pleasant but unyielding, not to be dissuaded. 'While you are here you are my responsibility,' he said calmly, in a voice which meant he didn't expect any further argument. 'And as a Northlander I consider it my duty to see that you leave us with as high an opinion of the area as it's possible for you to have.'

And spoiled the pompous remark by tossing her a teasing grin. Lora felt winded. She would never be able to understand him!

However, she learned a lot more in the days that followed. He seemed to relax, as though somehow she had passed some esoteric test, and she discovered that he could be a fascinating companion, possessed of a dry wit that occasionally was biting but more often amused. He worked harder than anyone else at Kahurangi, spending hours in the office, yet there wasn't a job he couldn't do on the station, from shoeing the horses to felling trees in the woodlots.

Lora found herself liking him, and was pleased, because liking was an emotion she could deal with. If she could see him as a friend, the wild undertones of attraction were diluted, easier to suppress. It made it easier when he went away; for the few days he was in Auckland she could persuade herself that the wildfire attraction was nothing, that there were no banked embers of desire, merely the casual magnetism of virile male for nubile woman.

She almost managed to convince herself. When he came back, the pleasant camaraderie had gone; he was aloof and abstracted. Lora wondered if he had a mistress in Auckland, and was appalled at the spark of jealousy that burned through her mind.

It encouraged her to sublimate her chaotic thoughts in work, dealing with the several government departments who had to be consulted about planning for the field day. It was interesting and testing; frequently she had to call on all her skills as an organiser, and occasionally as a mediator.

One morning, after receiving three telephone calls from an increasingly curt under-secretary, she went into the kitchen. Jane was making bread, plump arms working smoothly and strongly as she kneaded. She looked up and smiled. Still not exactly friendly, now that she had seen that Lora was not going to make a nuisance of herself over Matt, she was beginning to relax her aloof stance.

'Is there anyone about who can take a message to Matt?'

Jane continued expertly working the bread. 'No. Is it important?'

Lora lifted a brow. 'Yes,' she said simply.

The housekeeper nodded. 'Well, if he's not answering the walkie-talkie you'd better take the Land Rover and go and see him. He's mustering the deer.'

'Yes, I know.' Lora stood indecisively for a moment, her blonde head tilted a little, then said on a note of resignation, 'I suppose I'd better. A plague on all bureaucrats, I say.'

Jane chuckled. 'That isn't what Matt says.'

Lora smiled. When confronted with the convolutions of government protocol, Matt's vocabulary tended to be earthy and more than direct. 'Well, his wording might be different, but the sentiment's the same.'

He had insisted that she take the Land Rover for a test drive only the day before, sending her out with Jane's husband along the road, which she now knew was called the race, that ran through the entire station, and he had accepted her mentor's decision that she was perfectly capable of getting the thing from A to B with a smile that suggested he had had no qualms.

Lora had not been quite so confident, so it was with a frown of concentration that she turned the key. Once started, however, she relaxed, enjoying the sensation of being on her own for once. An essentially solitary person, she was always content with her own company, and living in a house with others around most of the time was a strain.

The race crossed the bridge just above the waterfall, noisy after a night of rain, then wound through the hills towards the back of the station, up a steep rise with magnificent views over the bay and down into a secluded valley which had the telltale high netting fences denoting deer. They were notoriously flighty and easily alarmed, so she came down as quietly as she could, running to a smooth halt some distance away from the pens.

There were deer already in the yards; she couldn't see through the high, solid walls, but there were sounds of movement behind them, and a highly strung herd in the pen outside, great dark eyes watching her with every appearance of terror. Wondering just how to introduce herself without causing a panic, Lora hesitated a moment beside the vehicle, then firmed her chin and set off across the trampled grass.

A little sigh of relief escaped her when she saw a man swing over the top of the pens and down towards her, a sigh that evaporated when she saw it wasn't Matt but the manager of the deer stud.

She explained what she wanted and he nodded. 'I'll get him.'

A man of few words. A moment later Matt appeared, eyes narrowed against the sun. He had rolled his shirt-sleeves up and was clad in boots and a pair of faded moleskin trousers, as was the other man, who was almost as tall and as well-built. So why, Lora asked her heart, did it leap only at the sight of one man?

His teeth gleamed white in his tanned face as he smiled at her. 'What is it?'

She explained, and he frowned. 'Why won't they damned well consult each other, instead of ringing me all the time?'

It was a rhetorical question; he knew as well as she did that that was not the way things were done in Wellington. 'They'll have to wait until I've had time to make a decision,' he said. 'Tell them I'll ring them later today—around four, say. I'm not going to stop now.'

'Right,' she said, and began to turn away.

He waited until she had taken a couple of steps, then asked, 'Do you want to see what we're doing?'

Suspiciously, she countered, 'You're not cutting off the horns for velvet, are you?'

He laughed. 'No, we're not. These are last year's fawns that we're drenching against parasites. However, although the velvet removal isn't a pretty sight, I can assure you it doesn't hurt the animals. They're given a tranquilliser and an anaesthetic, and a vet is here all the time.'

She said, 'Oh, I'm sure you don't hurt them, but Tim told me what it looked like. Ugh!'

He gave her a sharp look. 'Tim,' he said, 'is prone to exaggeration, I'm afraid. In all areas of his life.'

It sounded like a warning. She moved a little uneasily, wondering if he knew that, far from being dissuaded by her flat refusal to join him in his little plan of revenge,

Tim lost no opportunity to coax her to go out with him. And when there were no opportunities he made them, arriving at odd hours and surprising her in odd places.

'Yes,' she said in a colourless voice, stooping to pet a dog. It offered her a welcome change of subject. 'I thought you didn't use dogs with deer?'

He followed her lead, although there was a cooling in his tone. 'This one is special, a very quiet little bitch who seems to know how to deal with them. I'm going to breed her, see if the quirk of character that makes her so good with them can be fixed in her progeny. That's how all the characteristics of our other breeds of dogs were fixed, so it should be possible to do the same with this one.'

'It sounds interesting.' Her fascination must have shown in her voice, because he smiled again.

Lora let out her breath. She would have to stop looking for those smiles. She was becoming too reliant on them, and she knew that that wasn't a sign of friendship. Friends didn't take away your independence.

Straightening, she said unevenly, 'I'd like to see what you're doing, thank you.'

Watching the two men deal with the flighty, jittery deer was fascinating. The drench was in a kind of gun affair and, as each animal in the narrow race, only wide enough for one, came up level with the man wielding the instrument, it was grabbed, head lifted and the gun inserted down the throat, all as deftly and quickly as a machine, with so little fuss that the animals seemed hardly to know what had happened.

Lora thought wryly that machines did not have the grace and strength of these men, or the muscles that played so freely beneath skin and material, the quiet competence that let each animal free before it had time to panic.

Still, she rejoiced with each small animal as it fled, released from a captivity all the more frightening because it would have no idea what it was for. Only those who had been captive could truly appreciate freedom.

Which was why she would have to forget that Matt Duncan made her stupid body sing, and her heart tremble. Instinct warned her that he was possessive. Oh, not in the pathological way of her father, insanely jealous of any other claim on his wife's affection, even that of their child, but possessive in a masculine way that would leave any lover of his in no doubt as to who was master in that relationship.

And she had seen what jealousy could do, had learned to despise her mother for not holding out, not rebelling. Once she had asked her why she put up with it, the accusations, the suspicion, the occasional violence, and had been told that it was because her husband loved her, and she, loved like that, could not leave him.

The adolescent Lora had decided that if that was what love was like she wanted nothing of it.

She had changed her mind, a little, when she had realised that none of her married friends seemed locked into such a situation, but the first time she had ever found a man she might have fallen in love with she had felt the stirrings of a jealous mistrust, and she had been appalled into cutting him from her life as swiftly as a king disposed of a rebellious lord in olden days.

Even now, watching Matt from beneath her lashes, she remembered how she had felt when Keren Smithers had draped herself over his arm. Sheer, savage resentment, dangerous, terrifying, humiliating.

She would rather die a virgin, never loved, never loving, than expose anyone else to that taint in her blood. Better never to free such an ogre from the bonds of restraint and discipline that she had caged it in.

Quietly, her face smooth as a mask, she turned and went out of the shed.

That night after dinner Tim came around and asked her to go to the cinema at the Waitangi Hotel. After a moment's hesitation, and impelled by memories of the way her heart had flipped when Matt smiled at her, she went with him.

It was a good evening, the film a comedy that made her laugh, and, although she wasn't surprised to see Keren Smithers walk in with her aunt, at least Tim didn't make it obvious that he had asked her only to make the younger woman angry.

There was a sticky moment afterwards when they met in the car park. Tim grinned, but he greeted them politely, and ignored Keren's spiteful query as to whether he had fallen off any more horses to ask her aunt whether she had heard from a mutual friend lately.

Mrs Smithers had, and had news to impart; under cover of her aunt's voice, Keren said acidly, 'Making hay while the sun shines, Miss Reynolds?'

Lora could be intimidating when she chose, as this time she did. 'Sorry?' she said, looking down her nose to excellent effect.

Handicapped by the necessity of keeping her aunt from hearing what she was saying, Keren nevertheless managed to inject her voice with a considerable amount of venom. 'You know what I mean. Enjoy it while you can. When you go back to Auckland, I'll still be here.'

And with rude determination she turned away from Lora and interested herself in what her aunt and Tim were saying.

Lora was silent all the way home, wondering whether perhaps Tim had misread the situation. There had been a note of something very like desperation in the younger woman's comments that alarmed her. Should she say something to Tim?

No, she had nothing sensible to say. But she needn't go out with him again. Keren was right; she was the outsider here, and would soon be gone.

Once back at Kahurangi, she let Tim escort her to the door and thanked him politely for a pleasant evening.

'Is that all you can say?' he asked in mock indignation. 'Pleasant? I'll have you know that women fight among themselves to go to the pictures with me. And you say thank you!'

Lora's chuckle was smothered by the pressure of his mouth. He took no notice of her stiffness and, as he was much stronger than she was and took his time making a leisurely exploration, she was forced to allow it.

Not that she objected too much. He kissed her with an enjoyment that was gratifying, and beyond the initial embrace he took no liberties. There was, she thought, something essentially wholesome about Tim. Lora relaxed and let him finish.

Unfortunately they were interrupted by the sound of footsteps on gravel. Intent on extracting the last particle of pleasure from his kiss, Tim didn't respond until Lora punched him in the ribs.

Then he lifted his head and asked in an aggrieved voice, 'What——?'

'Sorry.' It was, of course, Matt who spoke, and the word was delivered with a glacial emphasis which made Tim jump back as though he had been caught rustling deer.

'Er—we were just saying goodnight,' he said inanely.

'So I see.'

Lora's initial amusement disappeared. What right had he to sound so stuffy and embarrass poor Tim? She pulled away and smiled up into Tim's scarlet face.

Tim returned it, but infuriated her by saying earnestly, 'Er—I'd better go. Night, Lora. Night, Matt.'

'Goodnight,' she said sweetly. 'I'll see you in the morning.'

Tim scuttled away and Lora, back very straight, preceded Matt into the house. When, however, she would have gone on up the stairs, he said abruptly, 'Only a month ago Tim thought he was violently in love with Keren Smithers.'

Lora had set her foot on the first step. She turned, startled to find herself still shorter than he was. The anger in her eyes was matched in his; he was, she realised in astonishment, furious.

'So?'

'So,' he said silkily, 'he's hardly the constant type. He does, however, fall hard when he falls. Unless you want to make him a very happy man, I'd be grateful if you steered clear of him.'

The innuendo was plain. Lora's eyes iced over, but she said merely, 'Thank you for your advice,' before turning away and walking on up the stairs.

He didn't follow her, although she felt his stare boring into her shoulders until she reached the landing. Once in her room, she said something sharp and biting, then allowed herself the luxury of a few minutes hating Matt Duncan without wondering why she was so angry.

Her mind in a turmoil, she got ready for bed. Presumably he had come upstairs while she was showering, for when she lay stiff and resentful between the sheets she saw the glow on the curtain which told her that the light in his bedroom was on. It stayed on for about half an hour.

Lora welcomed the darkness; surely now she would be able to sleep? And indeed, she was just sliding into oblivion when there came a sharp rattle of gravel against her window.

She jerked upright. Silence, until it was broken by another scatter of small stones against the glass.

Wary yet compelled, she went across to the open window, pulled aside the curtains and looked out.

It was just light enough for her to recognise Tim when he stepped out of the shade of the jacaranda and gestured silently, beckoning her down. For a moment she hesitated, until, struck by something imploring in the silent figure below, she nodded and tiptoed across her room to pull on a pair of jeans and a cotton knit sweater. It was ridiculous to hold her breath all the way down the stairs, but she did, and stupid to jump when one of the hinges in the back door gave a soft shriek, but she was still shaking when Tim appeared out of the darkness in front of her.

'What do you want?' she demanded crossly.

He laughed, but she noticed he too kept his voice low. 'We didn't get time before, but I wanted to ask you what Keren said to you tonight.'

She didn't waste any time in recriminations. 'She said that when I had left she would still be here.'

'Hardly profound,' he complained. A grin broke over his face. 'Doesn't that seem hopeful? If she didn't care about me at all, she wouldn't warn you off, would she?'

'How do I know?' she returned grumpily. 'I'm going back to bed, and I suggest you do the same.'

'I couldn't interest you in a moonlight swim?' The laughter in his voice combined with a coaxing note that almost brought a smile in response.

Ruthlessly squashing it, Lora fixed him with her sternest look and said, 'No, you could not. As it happens, there isn't a moon tonight. Goodnight.'

He was still chuckling when she locked the door. She drew in a deep breath and leaned back against it, the key in her hand. Adrenalin joined with the frightening tide of restlessness to make her wide-eyed and jumpy. She would never be able to sleep if she went back to her room, so she waited until she guessed that Tim would be almost back at his quarters, and then slid noiselessly through the door and away from the house, down across the scented garden and over the paddock towards the beach.

It was a warm, dark night, yet so brilliant were the stars that she could see almost as clearly as if there had been a moon. A sudden frisson of delight caught her unexpectedly. She gazed up into a sky glittering with silver, and slowly the complex mixture of emotions that had sent her out into the night was replaced by awe, pure and simple, and a strange longing she had never known before.

Everything suddenly seemed very simple and very frightening. She was a tiny speck, lost in a vast, impersonal universe that was beautiful beyond understanding. Yet, insignificant though she was, she could look up at the stars and feel a kind of peace seep into the recesses of her soul. She stayed there for a long time, listening to the quiet noises of the night, watching the stars wheel along their immutable paths. Then she turned and, with the light of the stars sheening her hair to a silver nimbus, made her way back to the homestead.

The trek through the silent house to her bedroom was even more nerve-racking than the trip down. Lora was not normally nervous, but it seemed to her heightened senses that the whole homestead was holding its breath, waiting for Matt to come out of his bedroom and confront her with that searing contempt that flayed the surface of her soul.

But he didn't.

And eventually she slept, an enigmatic smile curling her full mouth.

Matt was very distant the next morning, but there was no sign of the contempt that hurt so much. Indeed, he saw little of her, as he spent most of the time out on the station, and when they did meet at mealtimes it was with a studied, impersonal coolness on both sides.

And, if Lora was affected by his withdrawal, she was too busy to brood. The next few days were hectic. The preparations for the party were finalised, and then one of the secretaries of one of the Ministers rang up in a panic—an Asian delegation couldn't get there until the day after the function.

'So?' Lora snapped, forgetting her usual calm secretary's voice.

'So they could quite possibly be offended if Duncan goes ahead and holds the shindig without them.'

Lora sighed, but accepted the realities of face and prestige. 'I'll see what I can do,' she said, resignation sharpening the words.

Fortunately, before she had rung the caterers, he rang back. They had managed to make other arrangements, and all was well.

And then it was all ready, and she was walking down the stairs, hoping to heaven that she had covered everything. However, she had no time to brood, for almost as soon as she arrived downstairs the first car came rolling down the drive, and after that she was too busy to think.

It was a wonderful party. Everyone assured her of that. Even Keren Smithers said so, although Lora took the throwaway comment with a large grain of salt. It had, she was sure, been made only because Mr and Mrs Smithers were standing right there beside her.

Lora felt sorry for her, especially when Matt kissed her cheek and the childish prettiness was irradiated by an excitement that owed nothing to childishness. But really, she thought savagely as she met Keren's smug blue glare, wasn't love supposed to make one a better person?

Fortunately she was too busy using her knowledge of languages to be irritated for long. The visitors spoke English well, but found the broad New Zealand accent of some of the guests confusing, so she had to keep fairly close to them most of the time.

After about an hour Tim arrived, sleek and well-tailored in a dinner-jacket that had clearly been made for him. Lora saw him looking around the room, and drew back behind a large woman in a stunning caftan of palest greens and milky silver who was the district's most creative weaver.

Too late. A moment later he arrived at her side, smiling with a wicked glint, and two glasses of champagne held in his hands.

'You look,' he said, handing her one with a bow which was a work of art, 'ab-so-lute-ly gorgeous. Grey silk—beautifully understated, very, very subtle, and a knockout.' He held his glass out and touched it very lightly to hers. 'Congratulations, ice maiden.'

Lora pursed her lips, but drank a small mouthful of the champagne, wrinkling her nose as the bubbles tickled.

'Not Matt's best,' Tim confided with a suggestive leer, 'but fairly close to it. Clearly the man wants to make sure his guests are having a good time. Oh, dear, look at poor little Keren!'

'Poor little Keren' was watching Matt as he spoke to a very seductively dressed redhead, her expression so belligerent that Lora quailed, sure that a scene was imminent. Sure enough, with a nasty twist to her lips, Keren set off across the room towards the two she was watching.

'Come on,' Lora said, stepping in her direction. Better for Keren to wreak her spleen on someone who was paid to take it than start a catfight with one of the guests.

Tim effectively stopped her flight by looping an arm over her shoulders and pulling her into his lean, rangy body. 'Listen, the silly little fool couldn't care less if the whole world sees how she feels about Matt. She's always got what she wants by grabbing and holding on, and she thinks that Matt will cave in just as her aunt and uncle always have. Only a good dose of humiliation will stop her from behaving like a spoilt baby.'

Which sounded rather as though he was seeing Keren with a clearer eye than before.

'Not here, if I can help it,' Lora said grimly, but she made no further effort to go across when she saw Mrs Smithers interpose herself between the two women.

Tim murmured entirely too close to her ear, 'Relax, lovely one—see what I mean? Aunty moves in immediately. They couldn't have any children, and when Keren's parents were killed they adopted her and doted on her to ruination. Honestly, they've bought her everything her spoilt little heart desired; I'm sure they'd buy Matt if they could.'

As if he had heard his name, Matt looked up. Lora felt the full cynical impact of his regard right down to her toes, especially the moment when his eyes came to rest on Tim's arm around her. Nothing moved in the handsome face, not a flicker of emotion, yet she felt as though she had been scorched through to the bones.

That look flustered her into indiscretion. 'Perhaps,' she said, waiting until Matt's attention had been claimed by one of the ministry types before she moved out of Tim's grip, 'perhaps he has plans for Keren. She's pretty and she knows the routine——'

'And she has the mentality of a greedy four-year-old.' Tim shrugged. 'Well, I suppose stranger things have happened, but I doubt it. Oh, she's pretty enough, and she's a hot little handful in bed, but Matt's not the sort to let his hormones rule his head. Too controlled, our local squire. Very cool. All those years he and Amber lived together, and still no one knows whether they were lovers.'

Lora wondered if he knew what he had just given away. A glance at his face revealed that he had spoken without thinking. She was just as much at fault, allowing herself to gossip about her employer, so she said hastily, 'It's none of our business, Tim.'

'Speak for yourself. Whatever Matt does is everyone's business around here!' He grinned recklessly and tossed off more champagne. Lora realised with dismay that he was more than a little drunk.

'Myself,' he continued cheerfully, 'I'd say no. I know Matt as well as anyone, and it seems to me that if he'd been the beauteous Amber's lover, Alex Stephanides for all his billions wouldn't have got the lady back. Just look at him, seething with charisma.'

Unwillingly, Lora's eyes drifted back across the room to where Matt was smiling down with immense charm into the bemused face of yet another attractive woman.

'All alpha-male,' Tim pointed out with a relish that didn't hide the hint of hero-worship. '*He* wouldn't have tamely let any woman he wanted leave him. Beneath that sophisticated charm there's a very dominating male. Besides, he had a couple of discreet but from all accounts very torrid affairs while she was in residence, and I doubt whether he would have if he had been bedding her. Matt demands loyalty, but he gives it too.'

Lora most emphatically did not want to hear any more of this. Even thinking of Matt making love to another woman made her heart feel as though it was being squeezed in a vice. Looking desperately around, she saw an elderly Thai gentleman standing alone. It was the perfect opportunity and she grabbed it, forsaking Tim, and for some while afterwards was kept very busy interpreting.

Towards the end of the evening she found herself alone, an empty glass in her hand, with a headache threatening. Everyone, as a quick glance around the room showed, was having a good time, a moderate amount of alcohol and the pleasant atmosphere having persuaded most that they could interpret for themselves. Even the most dutiful hostess could take a few minutes off.

CHAPTER FIVE

MOVING easily, without stealth, Lora walked out through the french windows on to the terrace. It was blessedly cool, even a little chilly, but she welcomed the flow of air over her heated skin. One hand tucked into place a strand of hair that had strayed from her classic chignon as she stepped across the stone to the balustrading. The sound of excited laughter lifted her head; Keren, she thought stolidly. Probably flirting with Matt.

A morepork called, lonely yet familiar, and further away a kiwi revealed the presence of a colony of the now rare birds in the forest at Waitangi.

Lora breathed in the salt tang, standing slender and straight, pale as a wraith in the silver and grey and black of the darkened garden. It was a night of utmost serenity, and she stood still, soaking it up, feeling a faint return of the peace she had encountered before in the night.

Long moments later, she sensed a change in the atmosphere, a thickening of the translucent clarity, and the hairs on the back of her neck rose in sudden, appalling fear. It was an effort to turn, but she did, staring into the dark façade of the house. Her eyes ached with the strain, but it wasn't until he moved that she saw him.

He had been standing in the deeper darkness of the chimney-breast, so completely hidden that the moon failed to catch the rich gleam of his hair, the snowy glimpses of shirt beneath the black formality of his dinner-jacket.

Primal fear caught in Lora's throat, lodged there and imprisoned her voice. She couldn't move, couldn't even force a whisper past the barrier in her throat, yet her brain was saying urgently, This is Matt! This is not some dark hunter of the night!

Her hand stole up to clench over the ridiculous thudding of her heart as if the rigid fingers could hold back panic. She said huskily, 'I—I didn't see you there.'

He continued his noiseless progress towards her. The crescent moon found him, caressing with probing fingers the warm tints of his hair, bleaching out all colour so that the golden man of her fantasies was now all black and silver, a beauty and a fierce danger made all the more potent because it was so seldom revealed. Stripped by the moon's unsparing light of the glowing hues of day, he was a forbidding figure, the severe lines of his features carved from granite; he looked as dangerous as any Viking warrior intent on plunder and slaughter.

The facile words died in her throat. Silently he came to stand in front of her; without a word he took the glass from her hand and put it on the balustrading. His fingers brushed against hers, warm and strong and implacable.

Why, she thought in panic as she stared, mesmerised, into the coldly slashed lines of his face, why did I lower my guard?

This was not the remote, cynical employer of the past days, the man she had begun to discount as any threat to her. Nor was it the man who had just once shown her an icy contempt that still ached in her bones when she recalled it.

She had made the classic mistake, allowing herself to be lulled, until she had forgotten that this was the man whose cruel vindictiveness had made it impossible for Sandy to get another job in New Zealand.

'I told you not to dazzle young Tim,' he said softly as his hand came up to cup her chin.

Scarcely aware of what he was saying, she shivered. 'I haven't——'

'Don't lie to me.' Not a hint of emotion ruffled the level voice. 'I hate liars.'

The smooth tone was the only warning she had; she could discern nothing in his eyes but a splintering confusion of icicles. She reached up to pull the intrusive hand away from her chin and began urgently, 'Matt, I——'

The eager words were stifled by the pressure of his mouth, cold as the wasteland in his eyes. Lora stiffened, and the brutal pressure eased, became seducingly sweet. For long seconds she held out against the potent sorcery, until at last it breached the barriers and the stiffness left her body and she sighed into his mouth, relaxing against his lean, powerful body in a surrender that revealed far more than she was aware.

The strong fingers under her chin lifted, slid the length of her throat to come to rest over the throbbing pulse at the base. Matt lifted his head and smiled as her heavy eyelids sank, and although she sensed the anger still in him, it was clear that for the moment he had it well under control.

'You knew that I wouldn't allow you to flirt with anyone else but me,' he said, very low.

Disappointment, fierce as a summer storm, pulsed through her. She glared at him from eyes pale as a cat's, heedless of what she was giving away. 'Why? Don't tell me you still believe in the *droit du seigneur*!'

He laughed, not trying to hide the satisfaction in his voice. 'Why not? I rather like the idea of bending you to my will, even if it's only for one night. Although I don't think I'd be happy to hand you over to another man afterwards.'

His nearness, the musky, compelling scents of his hair and skin, the soft warmth of his breath across her face, the hard expectancy of the lean body against her, all combined to confuse the usually logical processes of her brain. She tried to step away, but the arm across her back didn't relax, and when she looked indignantly up he was smiling again, the mocking, assured smile of a man who knew just how attractive he was.

A stab of emotion pierced Lora's heart. She thought it was anger and said stiffly, 'Let me go, please. I can't say I blame your previous secretary for thinking that her pursuit was welcomed, if this is how you behaved with her.'

She felt laughter lift his chest before she heard it. 'My previous secretary got no such encouragement, as you're well aware. This has been brewing from the first time we set eyes on each other.'

'And we both knew it was a bad thing.' It was no use denying it. 'You warned me off——'

'I think I knew even then that I was trying to escape the inescapable. This has been inevitable from the moment we looked at each other and somehow knew that together we'd make the moon cry with envy.' He bent his head and touched her mouth in a kiss light as a snowflake, holding her with his sure, confident hands as she shivered silently in an aching sweetness she had never experienced before.

But she rallied, pulling out some shreds of resistance from deep in her will. 'Nothing is inevitable.' Was that her voice, weak yet huskily sensuous? Swallowing, she tried again. 'Matt, this is not sensible. Let me go and we'll forget...'

His mouth on her forehead was warm and slow and sure. 'Forget? Do you think you can forget this, my sensible Lora? I don't, and I know damned well that I won't. You've found your way through my skin and into my bloodstream. You've been driving me mad for weeks; I've watched that pretty, controlled mouth and wondered time after time how it would feel soft and abandoned under mine, whether you taste as sweet as you look, and just what goes on in that poised, regal head of yours. And because it was the sensible thing to do, because I thought I didn't want any complications, I held back. I'm damned if I know why. I am going to find out just what makes you tick, lady.'

'I don't want——'

'Liar,' he interrupted, his voice hardening. 'Don't ever lie to me, Lora. You do want, just as much as I do. You wanted me five minutes after you got here, when I caught you looking at me as though you couldn't bear to be in a bedroom with me and not use the bed. I knew then that the mask of aloofness you wear would come off for me.'

The blatant arrogance brought her head indignantly up. 'If you think that all you have to do is kiss me a couple of times and I'll fall into your hands like a ripe peach, let me tell you I'm not so easily seduced!'

'I know,' he murmured, laughter almost concealing a note of wonder in the deep voice. 'One of these days you're going to tell me why you keep such a guard on your face, on your tongue, on your actions, but for now just remember that I can get behind it whenever I want to.'

As if to emphasise the arrogant certainty of his words, he kissed her, his mouth moving over hers until the tide of sweetness rolled over her and she opened her lips to the demand of his. Drowned in sensation, she could feel the erratic beat of the heart in her throat, but closer, more potent by far was the scent of him, warm and spicy and masculine, as potent and primeval as the odours of musk and ambergris, the heavy, erotic scents of jasmine and clematis that mingled in the moondappled air...

Until she had decided that there was never going to be a man who could overcome her fears of commitment, and so had stopped accepting invitations, she had been kissed quite frequently. Always before, she had been vaguely repelled by the ardour, by the physical closeness of the man who embraced her. Always before, her mind had been totally untouched, able to stand back and observe the situation, its cool logic unswayed.

But Matt was different. Repulsion was the last thing she felt. Reason surrendered to a far older, more powerful state. She was astounded and shocked to realise that her whole being was vibrant with a confusing mixture of emotions surfacing from some unknown part of her.

Beneath the warmth of his questing mouth, hers was tentative, almost hesitant, and when he explored the sweet depths she tensed, waiting for the tendrils of distaste to spoil the moment. But instead she felt a tingling begin in her breasts, tightening and pulling at the nipples in some mysterious alchemy until they were unbearably sensitive.

Sheer astonishment brought a soft whimper to her throat. He made a harsh, impeded sound and moved so that the hard muscles of his chest brushed against her breasts. A shaft of fire streaked through her body, pulled at her stomach and then at the sensitive fork of her body; a shudder rippled over her skin. The combination of sensations made the hair on the back of her neck prickle.

Oh, she thought, her last coherent thought, I can't bear this!

As if she had sent him a signal, the quality of the kiss changed. Instead of the gentle, almost teasing pressure, his mouth hardened, became fierce and demanded a response from her.

Flames licked through her body. She pressed herself into him—and froze.

The urgent pressure against her softness suddenly wiped the wantonness from her body as though it had never existed. He wanted her, and the knowledge was frightening, because her instincts were telling her that Matt Duncan was not like the other men who had wanted her, easily dismissed, easily forgotten.

He was a danger she could not afford to confront.

She pulled back, tearing herself from his arms in an agony of self-recrimination, stumbling in her need to be free of the perilous sweetness of that embrace.

He let her go, standing a few steps away while she tried frantically to regain some control of the normal processes of her body. Her breath came in feverish gulps, her heart was thundering out of control and she didn't know whether she was hot or freezing, only that her skin was prickly with sensation.

In fact, it was only after she had shaken her head several times that she heard his voice, and she was in such a state that she didn't fully appreciate that it too revealed a shaken astonishment.

'Lora,' he said unevenly, and when she didn't answer he said, 'I knew that it would be—unusual, you're an unusual woman, but I assure you I hadn't—I didn't—I don't normally act with such—so rashly.'

Her voice was husky and strained. 'I don't believe you. I——'

The words trailed into silence. Shivering, she put up a hand to her hair and bit her lip in a frantic attempt to keep it from trembling.

'Lora!' He touched her arm, and when she flinched away from him he swore under his breath and tightened his grip, turning her so that he could look into her face.

She knew what he saw. Tears trembled on her lids, making her eyes seem larger and more luminous in the pale length of her face. Her mouth was soft and red, blurred by the passion of that last kiss.

'Hell,' he said, and surprisingly pulled her into his arms and held her there in an embrace which was pure comfort. It was dangerously easy to lean into his protective strength, to be supported and shielded.

So she pulled herself away and ran a shaking hand down her dress, straightening the material as though it were all that mattered.

'I'm sorry,' Matt said evenly, 'for behaving like a boy on his first kiss, totally at the mercy of his hormones. The only excuse I can give is that we appear to create some pretty explosive chemistry together.'

'It's all right,' Lora muttered.

'It is not all right.' He sounded angry. 'Why do I get the idea that I shocked the hell out of you?'

'I don't know.' Pride stiffened her neck. 'Perhaps because whatever you do in your vast experience of women, I'm not accustomed to acting like a hussy.'

He laughed through his teeth. 'Hussies went out in Victorian times, my dear.'

'Possibly, but putting a pretty name on it doesn't sweeten the act.'

'I wonder if you know how bigoted you sound. A kiss, that's all it was. Even the most rigid moralist would think twice about consigning us to hell on the strength of one kiss. After all, I feel quite certain that young Tim gets more than one kiss from you on those nights when you sneak out of the house to meet him.'

Pain, sharp as a lance, speared through her heart. But of course that was all that it was to him, a kiss. No matter that in his arms she had felt for long moments the ecstasies of paradise, he was able to dismiss the most exciting experience in her life with a few cutting words. And then she realised what he had said.

Her head whipped around, all softness gone from her face. In the moonlight her eyes were pale and cold, startling in the thick, dark beauty of her lashes. The silver light sheened across her face, emphasising the strength and purity of the foundation beneath the fine thin skin, and the icy composure that distanced him from her.

'Tim kissed me once,' she bit out with cold insolence. 'That same night he called me down on an entirely unrelated matter. I waited until he had gone and then went for a walk. By myself. Now, if you'll excuse me, I'm feeling rather cold and I'd like to go in.'

He said smoothly, not even trying to hide his disbelief, 'You should have said so before. I wouldn't have kept you out here if I'd known you weren't enjoying yourself.'

As a parting shot it couldn't have been bettered. He waited so that Lora could go in front of him, and made some innocuous comment about the moon on the pink and white flowers of the jasmine, a comment to which she dredged up a reasonably rational reply, so that when sharp eyes watched them come back into the room they appeared to be completely at ease with each other.

But in her bed that night, when at last she was able to take refuge there, she wept and thought that she would never again be able to smell the musky scent of jasmine without feeling both the shattering tide of need, and the sick humiliation that had followed.

After that, the field day was easy. She might have been upset if someone had dropped a bomb on the woolshed, but nothing short of that would have had the power to move her. She must have been her normal efficient self; in fact, she knew she was, because several people praised her for it. Even Matt, with the frost settled in his eyes, complimented her on her hard work and help.

But Lora had retreated too far into her shell to be reached by compliments, especially those delivered with glacial remoteness. Shocked and dismayed by her incandescent response the night before, she had pulled back into a calm composure which was as hard to pierce as armour-plating.

And two mornings after the field day, the morning after everyone had gone home, she came down the stairs with her barriers very carefully in place. She had another two days' work to do, and then she would be able to go back to Auckland. All she had to do was make it through the next two days.

The imperative summons of the telephone made her miss a step. She picked up the receiver, her secretary's voice, which until so recently she had thought was her true voice, to the fore.

It was Meri, speaking so quickly that for a few seconds Lora couldn't understand what she was saying.

'Slowly,' she implored, 'Meri, I can't——'

'Whales. Blackfish.' Meri drew a deep breath. 'Lora, there's a pod of whales in the bay, heading straight for the beach below the woolshed. They're going to strand themselves!'

Lora's fingers tightened painfully on to the receiver. 'What can we do?' she asked stupidly.

'Tell Matt. I'll round up anyone who can come and get down there, just in case we're needed.'

Lora ran out to the kitchen, aware that Jane would know where Matt was. However, she didn't need to ask because he was there too, sitting at the table drinking coffee.

'—so I said that I would have to wait—merciful heavens, Lora, what's the matter?'

At the first change in the housekeeper's voice Matt had looked up sharply; one glance at Lora's face brought him to his feet. 'What is it?' he demanded sharply.

All awkwardness forgotten, she told him, and saw the cloak of icy control drop away to reveal the disciplined force which lay at the heart of the man. Within seconds she was on the telephone to the Department of Conservation, warning them of the possibility of a stranding, and to the police and the local branch of the SPCA, while Matt set in motion his staff.

It took only a few minutes; when she put the receiver down for the last time Lora ran out on to the terrace and stood beside Matt, straining her eyes seaward. Sure enough, there were the dark shadows of the whales, too many to count, still forging steadily towards their doom on the beach. A small boat was at the head of the band, trying desperately to turn them away from the fatal shore, but even from the terrace it was obvious that there was no hope.

'Oh, why do they do it?' she whispered, appalled at the tragedy unfolding before their eyes, assailed by such a sensation of helplessness that she ached with it.

'No one knows.' Matt set down the binoculars with a thump. His mouth was hard, the slashing profile carved in formidable lines. He looked down into her anguished face and ordered, 'Go and get changed into warm trousers and top. It's going to be a long, wet business getting them off. Wear as much wool as possible. Then help Jane load the trailer with as many rags and sacks as you can find.'

Lora turned to go, unable to watch the actual process of stranding.

When she arrived down at the beach it was to find that the lead whale, impelled by some lethal compulsion, had beached, followed by about half the pod, who were lolling helplessly on the bottom, bewildered yet determined. The rest of the whales, all sizes from huge to pathetically small, milled around in water which grew shallower by the minute as the tide pulled inexorably out.

'Wet the sacks,' Matt commanded, 'and drape them over the whales. We have to keep them wet and as sheltered from the sun as possible. Don't block the blowhole, that's where they breathe, and for goodness' sake don't tip water down it. Come on—there's a good chance of saving most of them if we work quickly.'

What followed was a nightmare of effort, of organising a bucket brigade to keep the great creatures saturated with sea water, of trying to calm them. Matt worked like a demon in the hot sun, organising, exhorting; he didn't come near Lora, but once Lora saw him hug Keren, who was weeping at the distress of a baby as its mother tried vainly to reach it across the sand. He looked, she thought wearily, like a man with a mission.

But when Keren looked like continuing to cry he said something to her; she pouted, then looked about. Lora's eyes fell; she felt like an eavesdropper.

And she was extremely startled when Keren appeared to help the whale next to the one Lora already thought of as her special responsibility.

'Awful, isn't it?' Keren said chattily. 'Matt rang me up specially to come. I'm very good with animals.'

Lora said, 'There are enough of them about for you to be good with.'

But Keren was no more immune to the distress of the great creatures than anyone else. Within minutes she stopped trying to score off Lora and was busy soothing and caring for 'her' whale.

People appeared from everywhere, holidaymakers, locals, the officers from the Department, and too soon, it seemed, reporters and photographers who filed copy and then came back to help.

And all the time the inexorable tide sank lower and lower.

Drenched by seawater, Lora must have been cold, but she had no awareness of it. Her whole consciousness was bent on the whale so that the weary hours of wetting it, talking to it in soothing encouragement, waiting for the tide to turn so that the returning waters could ease the weight that was suffocating the animal, stretched on for eternity, yet passed quickly by.

Strangely, the whales seemed to understand that help was being offered. Whenever Lora spoke to hers the large dark eye looked intelligently at her, as though they shared a universal form of communication, one that crossed the boundaries of the species.

At one stage she discovered that she was weeping softly over their plight: the lords of the sea, so proud and gentle, so pathetically helpless now. Although they must have been close to panic throughout all those long hours they lay quietly, their great bulk quiescent as people scurried around them doing all the things that were necessary to keep them in good health for the returning tide.

Only the babies, calling in their panic, made any protest, but that was heartrending, and each time the boats out in the bay had to prevent the great adults still free in the water from forcing themselves on to the pitiless beach to come to the aid of the infants.

Some time after the men from the Department of Conservation arrived Lora heard the engine of one of the big farm tractors and saw that one of the farm gates had been converted into a sort of cradle.

Next to her, Keren asked, 'What are they doing?'

Someone a little further along replied, 'They'll try to get the leading whale on to it and take it out to sea. Sometimes it works.'

Unspoken was the fact that more often than not the whale, compelled by some unknown death-wish, turned obstinately back to shore.

The sun gleamed on Matt's hair as he watched the tractor being driven across the beach; like most of the men there, he had stripped off his shirt to drape one of the whales, and the muscles of his shoulders moved in a splendid symmetry of power beneath the smooth, tanned skin.

Conscious of Keren's eyes on her, Lora swallowed, and leaned a moment against the bulk of 'her' whale. The flippers made a harsh scraping sound in the sand; although it stung her already abraded skin, she used her hands to deepen the pits she had made to accommodate the flippers, then straightened to run her hand over the sack once more. The sun was now beating ruthlessly down; perfect holiday weather, she thought on a sob of frustration.

The sacking was already almost dry. And the tide was well out. If she left the whale to get water it would tip over on to its side and possibly suffocate before she could get back to it.

Impulsively, she called out to a man who was making his way towards them, asking urgently, 'Will you get a bucket of water, please?'

'Anything for you,' he said, his mouth twisting.

Lora stared; it took her a moment to realise that it was Gavin Browning.

'What are you doing here?' she asked stupidly.

He grabbed a bucket and over his shoulder replied with curt insolence. 'Oh, the agency hasn't sent me to check up on you, don't worry. I did tell you I was coming up here on holiday, but of course you didn't remember.'

Lora almost liked him for coming along to help, wishing that the personality clash which made him harass her was not so strong. But she emphatically did not want him here; he knew, none better, that she was Sandy's sister, and although he wouldn't deliberately spill the beans he might give something away. She looked over at Keren, but the other woman was bending down, her face and body turned away. She wouldn't have heard what had passed between them.

Gavin was back within minutes. 'Where do you want this?'

'Not near the blowhole,' she said swiftly. 'Wet the sack.'

He nodded and began to pour carefully so that the salt water dripped slowly over the material. Beneath Lora's hand the animal's skin turned from dry and hot to smoothly slick. She thought she saw appreciation in the liquid eye of the whale, and could have wept.

'Here,' Gavin said roughly, 'you look exhausted. Someone's serving tea a little further up on the beach. I'll support it while you go and get yourself a cup.' And when she hesitated he said angrily, 'I won't hurt it.'

'I know.'

He smiled without humour into her shocked face. 'You must have changed your mind a little about me, then. Go on, you won't be any use to it if you collapse.'

Reluctant to leave him there with Keren, she hesitated, then shrugged wearily and stepped back. What did it matter? Her concerns were hardly life and death matters. He was quite right; she would be no use to the whale if she weakened herself through dehydration or hunger.

Jane had set up a kind of mobile kitchen under the shade of one of the big pohutukawa trees, and she and a couple of other women were offering tea and cold drinks as well as huge sandwiches to those who needed them.

'Here,' Meri said, pouring tea into a paper cup. She had brought down the playpen, and in it sat a pleased but astonished Moana. The child's huge, dark eyes watched fascinated as the normally deserted beach seethed with life and activity. 'How's it going?'

Lora looked down at her scratched hands, the salt drying in an itchy film over the brown length of her legs. 'Not too bad,' she said.

Meri smiled. 'I think Moana's the only one who's really enjoying it. She loves excitement.'

'Where's Pete?'

'With his daddy.'

But Matt came up and deposited a reluctant Pete next to his sister. 'Stay there and be a good boy,' he commanded, and Pete's indignant protests died. To Meri, Matt explained, 'We need Rod to drive the tractor, so Pete will have to stay here for a while.'

'What's happening?'

He looked at Lora a moment before saying heavily, 'I'm going up to get the rifle. We're going to try and float the leader out, but if it's too disorientated we'll have to kill it. When a beaching happens the leader is usually sick and disorientated. Unfortunately the others won't leave it until it dies.'

Blindly, Lora put out her hand, her face stiff and immobile with the effort to contain her distress. To her surprise he took it, holding it against the warm, rough skin of his chest. Curtly, he said, 'If it has to be done, the sooner the better.'

'I know,' she said.

He looked at her a moment, his brilliant eyes scanning her face with a slow, penetrating gaze, then he smiled, an odd little twist to his lips, and said softly, 'When you forget to don that armour, you have such gentleness in your eyes and mouth. My sweet Lora.'

Bemused, her heart singing, she watched him as he turned to go, only gradually becoming aware of the others around.

And Meri's voice. 'Oh-oh, here comes trouble,' she muttered.

Trouble was Keren, but beyond imperiously demanding a long, cold drink she said nothing to anyone, keeping her face resolutely turned away from Lora, whose delight at Matt's unexpected gentleness was tempered by a strong sense of unease.

She drained the tea and set off back towards her whale, made uncomfortable by a sharp prickling between her shoulderblades. Keren watched her all the way down the beach.

Gavin was talking to the whale, his voice soothing and persuasive. When Lora appeared he almost jumped and said with awkward haste, 'It seems to comfort it.'

What a pity he tried to hide that unexpected softness! Lora gave him a warm smile and said, 'Yes. They really do seem to know we're trying to help, don't they?'

He nodded and moved away, watching critically as she took as much of the weight of the big creature as she could. 'Someone said they need help with the leader,' he said at last. 'I'll go and see if they need me.'

She said softly, 'Thank you, Gavin.'

He shrugged. 'Oh, I'd do the same for any whale.'

The attempt to move the leader was a failure. For long moments after the tractor had towed it out into the water everyone held their breath. At first it seemed that it might have succeeded, for the other whales met it with every appearance of delight. If only it stayed, the stranded ones could be refloated on the now rapidly gaining tide.

A collective sigh of pain and frustration sounded from the beach as the huge creature turned and swam straight back on to the sand, causing chaos in those animals that were still swimming. The flotilla of small boats managed to prevent all but three from following it, but it was a near thing, and it was clear that they were not going to be able to hold them there for much longer.

With tears rolling down her cheeks, Lora saw a grim Matt take the rifle. She closed her eyes at the crack of the weapon, burying her face in the wet sacking as two other shots followed. Beneath her, the whale quivered.

And then it was over. Biting her lip savagely, she watched as Matt and the Ministry of Conservation official walked back across the beach. She knew exactly how Matt was feeling: the frustration and anger, the impotent fury at a malevolent fate that had made him an instrument of death.

Yet the set of his shoulders was just as erect, his stance as smooth and free from stress.

Not a man it was easy to know; certainly, no one looking at the grim mask of his features would be able to tell just how much that deed had hurt. And it was like him to do it himself rather than foist it off on to anyone else.

But it seemed as though the slaying of the lead whale had done the trick. As the water lapped in, one by one the others were freed, gently shepherded out to their waiting companions, and although there was a certain amount of milling about and confusion, and one or two moments when everyone stood tense and fearful because it looked as though their charges were hell-bent on destroying themselves, the whales stayed out beyond the waves.

Lora wished hers good luck, feeling a surge of choking emotion in her throat. It seemed to look at her, then the great muscles moved under the dark skin and it was in its native element and she waved, watching as the pod reformed and turned slowly towards the east and the open sea. Matt strode away from the enthusiastic watchers, many of whom wept openly, and went down the sand to where his runabout was waiting. With the other boats, he would accompany the whales until they were well out of the bay that had trapped them.

A ragged cheer lifted Lora's head. It wasn't until she saw the tears on Meri's cheeks that she realised that she was crying, too.

'Come on,' Jane Crawford said, ever practical. 'I've made a great pot of soup; you're all welcome to come up to the homestead and get warm.'

Many went straight home, but a surprising number of damp, sandy, exhilarated whale-rescuers ended up in the big kitchen drinking soup and eating hot rolls while they discussed the day's events; almost, Lora thought, as though they were on too much of a high to be able to come down easily.

Gavin was one of them. Silent, not responding to Keren's rather obvious overtures, he leaned against the wall, watching the others and making Lora profoundly uneasy.

At last she slipped out of the room, intending to shower away the salt and grime, but he followed her and said, 'I want to talk to you.'

Frowning, she opened her mouth, but he forestalled her objection. 'Here will do.'

She saw his determination in his expression and sighed and said, 'Come into——'

'Outside.' He looked around with envious rancour. 'You fit very nicely into such blatant opulence, but it makes me feel sick. Too rich for my taste. We'll go for a walk in the garden.'

She nodded and preceded him out on to the terrace and down the steps. Some suppressed emotion in his attitude warned her that she was not going to enjoy what he had to say to her, but she had been dealing with him for long enough not to be unduly upset. There was nothing Gavin Browning could do to hurt her.

He stopped beneath one of the jacarandas, its buds swelling into a faint purple haze, but she said, 'Not here, Gavin. There's a seat a little further on...'

Stupidly, she was sentimental about the jacaranda from which she had watched Matt riding in the moonlight.

Backed against a thick hedge of sasanqua camellias, the seat was surrounded by a paved area where a small daisy plant flowered in clouds of pink and white. Lora sat down and waited for Gavin to sit before asking with a hint of impatience, 'What do you want?'

'Now there's an opening,' he returned with a mirthless smile.

Lora's face mirrored her distaste. 'Be sensible.'

'Well, that's the problem. I don't think I can.' He watched her puzzled expression for a few seconds before saying smoothly, 'Your neighbour at the whale hospital informed me that you are making a nuisance of yourself over Matt Duncan.'

CHAPTER SIX

LORA was not surprised. Somehow she had guessed. Curbing the desire to tell him exactly what she thought of Keren, she retorted trenchantly, 'If that was so, he'd have sent me on my way weeks ago. Did she also tell you that she is in love with him?'

'No.' He looked at the flaxen wisps of hair at the tender nape of her neck; his mouth tightened. 'She didn't have to. I saw for myself. Are *you* in love with him, Lora?'

'That is no one's business but mine. You can be quite sure that the agency has no need to worry about my not doing my job.'

'We were sure of that with Sandy, too.'

His voice was too level. Stricken, she felt his malice as if it were a blow, one from which she could not defend herself. The colour rolled back from her skin, leaving her ivory and silver, her eyes bleached of colour.

He said in that same even voice, 'I hope you're telling the truth, Lora. It would be a pity if you followed your brother out of the agency.'

'Are you threatening me?'

'No,' he said quietly. 'I'm warning you, Lora. Sandy fell in love with the woman who betrayed him. I wouldn't like to see it happen to you.'

She looked at him, really looked at him for perhaps the first time in years, and felt as though she had been blind all that time. Perhaps she had always known that he was in love with her; perhaps they had both used their dislike as an armour. Perhaps... but it was too late now.

She could never love him, because she had given her heart away to a man who did not value it. And she would not let Gavin see that she had discerned his secret. Let him keep his pride; he was not likely to get anything else from her.

'It won't,' she said, the truth ringing hard through the promise.

He nodded. 'When are you coming back?'

'At the end of the week.'

'I'll see you then.'

And he was gone, striding off through the garden.

Lora sighed, then got to her feet and walked back into the kitchen to find that most of the helpers had gone, leaving only the most determined to drink tea and carry on rehashing the day's events.

She looked around, smiling and nodding at the few she knew. No Keren, she was glad to see. She must have taken herself off. Not before time, malicious little monster. Just as well she had gone.

If only the others would!

But at last they too left, and she and Jane looked at each other across the big room, each face wearing the same resigned expression.

'Well, I must say I'm glad to see the last of them,' Jane said, picking up two large mugs from the table. 'You look worn out; why don't you go and tidy up?'

Lora shook her head, trying to blink away the beastly combination of grit and heat from her eyes. 'I'll help,' she said, viewing distastefully the remains of a bread roll.

And in spite of Jane's protests she did, wondering as she stacked the dishwasher whether the whales had left the bay or whether the fatal compulsion that had brought them in was still working its mysterious siren's spell on the leaders.

And whether Matt was still as untiring as he had been all day, or if that magnificent vitality had at last faded.

She recalled the moment when it had been decided to shoot the leading whale, and shivered. He had strength, and an icy determination that had accepted the necessity of killing; not many men would have shown so little

emotion at the bleak facts, or the cold strength needed
to dispatch the animal they had tried so hard to save.

He didn't come home; he radioed in to say that he
would stay with the pod for some hours to make sure
they remained at sea. Disappointment mingled with an
odd relief. Lora wondered whether she was making too
much of those precious moments when he had smiled at
her and she had thought she saw something perilously
close to tenderness warm his eyes.

Much later, after she had lain wide-eyed in her bed
for what seemed hours, she managed to drift off, but
something brought her awake with such a start that she
sat up hastily, her ears straining for the sound which had
woken her.

Nothing, and no repetition of it, either. She turned
her head, anxiously searching the room. A glance at the
luminous dial of her clock revealed that it was almost
two o'clock in the morning. Apart from the soft whispering of the wind in the branches of the jacaranda and
the muted lullaby of the waves, she could hear nothing.

Yet something compelled her to her feet and across
the room to the door. She opened it, holding her breath
as she saw light from below seeping up the stairs. For a
moment she hesitated, made craven by old fears, then
set her shoulders and walked softly along the Persian
runner and down the staircase.

The muted glow came from the half-opened door of
the office; again she hesitated, but it was probably a
lamp left on, no more. Stepping silently, she went in.

Sure enough, it was the lamp beside the armchair.
Laughing silently at herself for allowing fantasies to
frighten her, she went across the room, bending over the
chair to turn the lamp off before she realised that Matt
was sprawled in the chair, his face unguarded in sleep,
set in lines of exhaustion. He had showered but not
shaved, and the dark gold shadow about his lean jaw
gave him a piratical air, swashbuckling and sensuous.

He seemed to be clad only in a blue towelling robe that came half-way down his thighs.

Lora's eyes lingered on the long lines of his body, the strong muscles far from lax even though he was sound asleep. A little flame burned deep into her self-possession; an impeded sound escaped her as she went to straighten up, for his lashes flickered and he lifted heavy eyelids, smiling a little as his eyes met her wide, startled ones.

'Lora,' he said with satisfaction, and pulled her on to his lap.

She stiffened, but he laid his head on her breast and went back to sleep, nuzzling in for comfort as his hands relaxed, the long lines of his body settling into sleep.

It was perilously sweet to sit like that, sweet and forbidden, especially as she had not pulled on her dressing-gown and was dressed only in a white cotton nightgown that was demurely cut but thin. Still, although she told herself that she had to move, she stayed, torn by a complex of sensations that mirrored almost too exactly the confusion of her feelings.

The lamplight glowed richly on the tawny head at her breast, limning the leonine profile in gold. She felt a kind of maternal loving, a gracious, giving emotion, and with it, darkening it, a fierce, powerful possessiveness that both appalled and terrified her.

She bit her lip until it was white, held rigid by shock and pain. Was this the emotion which had driven her mother to make a fatal marriage, this potent amalgam of passion and possession? Was it this that had transformed her father from the bright, bold man Sandy could just remember to the domestic tyrant who had rendered all their lives hideous?

But, although the possibility rendered her panic-stricken, she could not move. Her eyes were trapped by Matt's face against her breast, her body held prisoner by sensations she had never before experienced. A slow, heated liquidity rendered her bones flaccid; as she watched in dismay, her nipples beneath the thin cotton peaked into tight, hard, unbearably tender nubs.

Matt's breath came hotly through her nightgown, setting off alarm bells through her entire system. She took a deep, jagged breath, but that brought her nipple into contact with his rough cheek; sensation, sharp and painful, incredibly arousing, thrilled through her. She felt a savage need in the pit of her stomach and heat in her cheeks, in her breasts, an aching, wanting emptiness that she savoured even as it set her body throbbing.

All her conditioning, every tenet on which she had built her life, insisted she flee now while she could, but an older, deeper instinct held her captive, her breath locked in her lungs, her heart pounding a tattoo of anticipation.

Matt moved restlessly, his hand coming unerringly to her breast. He smiled and said her name, and at the same time turned his head. His mouth touched the smooth, heavy curve of her breast before closing over the nipple so pleadingly near it.

A deep groan tore through Lora and she gasped, transfixed by a sensation so erotic that she thought she might die of it, be pierced through and through by delight until she was Lora no longer, just sheer sensation, woman trammelled by an unbearable pleasure.

But, even as her untutored body responded, she knew she had to leave before he woke, before the ravishment of his mouth stole her mind and her will away, leaving her bereft, only an instrument of his pleasure.

But oh, it took an effort of will to pull herself free, to ease herself from his avid mouth. She managed it, only to stare, horrified, at the way the wet cotton clung over her breast—it looked wanton, earthy, sensuous—everything that she had avoided in her life. Viciously she jerked the material away from her skin, as though by hiding the evidence of her body's betrayal she could banish the instinct that urged her surrender.

Shaking, her body trembling in a fever of turmoil, she began to ease herself off his lap; his hand at her breast tightened, and he said quite distinctly, 'No. Not yet!'

And then, as if the sound of his voice woke him, his eyes opened, and he was staring up into her horrified face.

The silence was terrible, heavy, ominous with unspoken thoughts. She felt the colour flee her skin, felt the heat he had engendered die in a smoking heap of ashes under the comprehension in his eyes.

But when he spoke the words astounded her. 'I should have known,' he said in a flat, hard voice. 'You have the same eyes as Sandy. You look just as he did when he admitted passing on information.'

So Gavin had told him.

Her face washed in shaming colour, she pulled mutely away. Instantly his hand left her breast to clamp around her elbow. At the cruel restraint she flinched, but her head lifted. She had done nothing wrong; she would not cower.

He looked up at her standing in front of him, the wet cotton pulling over her breast, and something ugly moved in his eyes.

Very softly, he asked, 'What is this all about, Lora? Why are you here?' When she made no answer, he finished in that voice of lethal smoothness, 'Did he want a little revenge for being caught in the act?'

Her throat was dry. She stood like a child caught in wickedness and she was unable to speak, unable to defend herself. For a second she was transported back to childhood and the old panic set her heart skipping, fluttering in impotent terror, because Matt was looking at her as though he would like to kill her.

He asked inexorably, 'Well, Lora? Is that why you're here? To use that delectable body to seduce me into falling in love with you? A little revenge for your brother?'

This released the floodgates. 'No!' And at the barest lift of an eyebrow she said, 'Sandy doesn't know I'm here!' That disbelieving brow rose a fraction higher. 'Surely Gavin Browning told you——' His expression didn't change, but she knew. Between her teeth she said, 'So it was Keren! The little bitch! She listened——'

'She overheard you talking to your lover in the garden, yes,' he said, watching her through narrowed eyes, 'and naturally she thought that I should know.'

'Naturally.' The irony was marked and acid. 'Perhaps she should have overcome her *natural* aversion to eavesdropping and listened a little less selectively, and she might have realised that, far from being my lover, Gavin Browning is my superior at the agency, and it is pure coincidence that he is up here on holiday.'

His lashes dropped. 'Indeed? I can't see why Keren should lie to me, and she seemed totally convinced of your relationship.'

'I wonder what gave her that idea?' Lora laughed angrily. 'Because I don't like him, and he certainly does not like me.'

'I see.' But what he saw she didn't know because his face was impassive, and with his eyes hidden she could not discern whether he believed her or not.

And suddenly it was extremely important that he did believe her.

But when he spoke, it was on a different subject entirely. 'Why did you find it necessary to come here under a false name?'

She was nonplussed for a second, her normally quick mind sluggish. But she recovered and said, 'It isn't false! Sandy is my half-brother. We had the same mother—different fathers.'

'So how did it happen that you just happened to turn up here on the heels of a man who sold information that lost me a packet of money? Looking to do the same, Lora?'

The cold, restrained menace in the calm voice made her shiver. He was looking at her with eyes that were flat and opaque, entirely without emotion, but she sensed the strength of the anger that lay just behind the barriers of his immense control.

Thrusting her chin forward, she said shortly, 'No. And Sandy did not sell your information. He was stupid enough to give it to the woman he assumed you were going to marry.'

'Hell hath no fury,' he murmured with a humourless smile. 'He broke trust.'

She went a little paler, if that was possible, but faced him staunchly. 'Yes, he did, and he regrets it very much, but that was no reason to hound him out of the country! You weren't content to have him sacked from his job, you had to make it impossible for him to get any work at all in New Zealand. Surely anyone who isn't an unreasonable tyrant must realise that everyone is entitled to one mistake!'

At the first intemperate words his lashes drooped, but not before she was pierced by a look of keen interest. 'Is that what he told you?'

She was already regretting her loss of control, but it was too late now. Shrugging, she said curtly, 'He didn't have to tell me. I work for the same firm, remember? I know what happened, and I know how miserable he was when he had to leave.'

'Most people feel quite miserable when they are found out in treachery,' he observed with hateful logic.

Lora took a step forward, only halting when those inscrutable eyes rested thoughtfully on the swift rise and fall of her breasts beneath the thin cotton. Colour stained her skin, but she didn't retreat. This could well be her only chance to help her brother, and she had to take it.

'Sandy may have been foolish, but he was not a traitor,' she said urgently. 'He did not sell those figures. He honestly thought that you were going to marry that woman. He had no reason to think otherwise. After all, you——'

She stopped precipitately.

'After all, she had been my mistress for several months,' he supplied, helpfully, after a tense few moments while she waited for the axe to fall.

She bit her lip and said nothing.

'So he didn't sell them?'

'No,' she said tiredly. Then, realising what he had said, she looked up with hope in her eyes. 'Do you believe me?'

'I believe that you believe he didn't,' he said, his gaze never leaving her face.

Disappointment flooded through her. 'Oh, why are you so suspicious and cynical?' she asked bitterly.

'Experience, my dear. By and large the world is full of people who sell themselves for various reasons. Money, security, sex... Sandy was in love with Claire, did you know that?'

She stared at him. 'Claire?'

'Claire Portsmouth. The woman scorned. He fell in love with her——'

'And if he did?'

A sardonic smile rendered the straight line of his mouth ugly. 'She was, of course, very pretty, in a sophisticated way. And experienced. More experienced than your brother, I imagine. He was really easy meat for her.'

She said uncertainly, 'If you understand that, why did you drive him out of the country?'

'What a melodramatic turn of phrase!' He was mocking her and she flushed, eyes shooting crystalline arrows at him until he continued, 'It didn't occur to you that he may simply have been unable to face what he had done, so he ran away?'

'Sandy is no coward,' she returned fiercely.

'No, of course not. Merely untrustworthy when it comes to a pretty face. Well, listen to this, Sandy's sister. I don't allow anyone to cheat me and get away with it!'

She stepped back, startled by the ferocity of the bald statement. At that moment she realised that the formidable presence of the man was based on an implacable authority, all the more concentrated because it was disciplined by an iron will.

'So, just to satisfy your pride, you made it impossible for him to stay in New Zealand,' she said painfully.

'I told his employers what he had done. And that I would not be using their services again while they had him on their wage list.'

Her expression hardened. 'And then you made it impossible for him to get another job in New Zealand.' She didn't know why it was important to her, but she wanted more than anything in the world for him to say that he had not hounded Sandy out of the country.

He watched her with a hooded stare. 'Would you believe me if I said no?'

She remembered Sandy's pain, his reluctance to go, his railings at Matt's vengeance. Just for a moment she wondered whether it had been his doomed attraction to Claire Whatever that had made him so bitter, but one look at the granite carving of the face of the man in the chair before her banished the suspicion. On his own admission he was a vengeful man. And into her brain came a picture of him as he had been when he'd shot the leading whale: calm, purposeful and relentless.

She suppressed a shiver and said quietly, 'No.'

'So, I stand accused as the man who drove your brother to flee the country. Where is he?' he asked in a voice of supreme uninterest.

She didn't trust him, but surely even Matt Duncan's arm couldn't reach all the way across the Pacific Ocean, so she told him, purposely omitting any other information.

'I hope he enjoys it there,' he said casually.

'He would enjoy it more at home.' Her bitterness showed in her tone.

'I'm sure he would. Tell me, just what would you be prepared to do to have me call a halt to this *vendetta* of mine?' His voice invested the word with a blighting sarcasm which did not register in his expression.

She stood her ground, her eyes scanning that suspiciously bland face. 'I don't know what you mean,' she replied slowly. 'The decision is yours.'

'Even such a vengeful character as mine could be persuaded to change its ways.'

Neither his cryptic tone nor the look on his face gave her any clue to his meaning. She said in bewilderment, 'I don't understand.'

'No?'

He didn't believe her, that was obvious, but as if the cat and mouse game he was playing had suddenly become boring his fingers tightened around her elbow and he jerked her off balance. She tried to break free, but he held her imprisoned on his lap, and when she felt the stirring in his thighs she gave a muffled gasp and stopped squirming to lift frightened, outraged eyes to the cold threat of his.

'Did you, by any chance, think that it might be easy to seduce me into easing the prohibition on your brother? As you are such a devoted sister?'

It took a moment for the insult to register, but when it did Lora went white, then scarlet, and her hand flew up. He had been watching, however, for before it had a chance to reach his face he imprisoned it in a cruel grip.

From beneath their half-closed lids his eyes gleamed, brilliant with some emotion she could not define. She was furiously angry, more angry than she had ever been in her life before, yet the sheer animal menace of the man held her still.

For a moment they were held in stasis like a tableau in a waxworks, the only movements a slow dilation of her pupils and the quick throb of a muscle beside his mouth. Then he forced her now reluctant hand upwards and held it to his cheek. His skin was abrasive, warm and tactilely stimulating against her palm; like cold jewels his eyes watched her reaction.

'So hot behind the icy composure,' he said reflectively. He smiled with a calculating charm which didn't warm his expression. 'A pretty little plot, Lora. I might be tempted to play. I think I'd rather enjoy being persuaded by you.'

Lora could no longer take refuge in protestations of not understanding, because his smile, the tone of his voice, the measuring assessment of his look as it dropped from her flushed, indignant face to the fall and rise of her breasts told her exactly what he meant.

Disgust, all the stronger because she felt a tiny blaze of sensation deep in her, warred with icy anger in her voice. 'Are you insinuating that I—that—how dare you?'

He laughed softly. 'How trite of you! It seems reasonable. After all, as all else has failed—your brother wrote, humbling himself to me, did you know?—the only thing left to do seems to have been to beard the lion in his den and use those abundant natural assets of yours to get what you want. Such a devoted sister!'

'You're paranoid,' she said, disgust a sharp thread through her voice.

'Hardly. Or only a little. You must admit it's stretching coincidence a fraction too far that you were the one who came up here. I'm sure there were others who would have been capable of doing the job every bit as well as you.'

'Not at all,' she said spiritedly. 'New Zealand is a small country. The others who could have done the job were already on assignment.'

'Or perhaps you persuaded Gavin Browning that you were the ideal person.'

She saw another danger, one that made her eyes darken with frustration. He had given Gavin's name an acid intonation that alarmed her and, although she did not like the man, she couldn't allow him to be stigmatised as part of a plot.

'If you ask Sheila Chester, the owner of the agency, you'll find that I'm right. Believe me, they didn't want to send me.' Anger got the better of her caution. 'But they wanted to lose the custom of the great and powerful and vindictive Matt Duncan even less! I didn't want to come, and I promise you I did *not* come up here to seduce you into letting Sandy come back!'

The patrician disdain in her voice caused a flicker in the dangerous glitter of his stare. His brows drew together as he appeared to be thinking. After a tense silence he said coolly, 'A pity. I'm willing to make a deal.'

Disappointment surged like a black flood through her. Striving desperately to hold her voice steady, she said, 'What sort of deal?'

His eyes gleamed with mockery. 'Oh, come now, Lora...'

Her breath caught in her throat. She tried to stare at him with her usual cold hauteur, but she was too vulnerable, her body too responsive and conscious of the nearness of his. She could see the tiny laughter-lines at the corner of his eyes, the hypnotic golden glow in the depths, the grainy texture of his skin roughened by the beginnings of his beard. He still held her capable hand against his cheek so that she was acutely aware of the contrast between her paler, finer skin and his. On her bare arm his hand made a striking statement, almost barbaric in intensity.

He smelt of his own special scent, warm male, erotic, evocative. And beneath her rigid body his legs were strong and powerfully muscled, his potent masculinity threatening her in a way she barely understood.

Colour seeped painfully through her skin. Hoping to shame him with the ugly truth, she tried to infuse her voice with contempt. 'Are you suggesting that if I agree to become your mistress you might allow Sandy to come back to work in New Zealand?'

His mouth twisted at the corner, but there was a watchfulness in his expression which warned her. 'Just that,' he said softly. 'It wouldn't be too difficult, Lora. We're dynamite together.'

'You have a bloody nerve,' she said in a trembling voice. 'How dare you think that I would prostitute myself for any reason? How dare——?'

His voice cracked through her protests with the stinging force of a whip. 'I dare for the same reason that you assumed, for no reason if what you say is true, that I would conduct a bitter vendetta against a man who had already paid for his transgressions by losing his job. What reason had you for tarring me with that sort of brush? What kind of man do you think I am? Your brother couldn't face the fact that he had been seduced by a slut into betraying his trust, so he ran all the way to Canada.'

She whispered, 'No, no, he didn't,' and he snarled something, then suddenly jerked her head back and silenced her with a kiss as searing as the contempt in his words.

He was angry and aroused, intent on forcing her to submit to the force of his male aggression, and she resented it, resented the smothering intensity of the kiss, resented futilely the way he stamped his possession on her, holding her captive in an embrace which revealed only too clearly that he was avid for her. She hated most the sudden wildfire exhilaration that sang through her blood, sweeping away the years of conditioning in a passionate response to a man who despised her. For he was not wanting her, Lora; he had made obvious what he thought of her, so the desire feeding so hungrily on her kisses was an impersonal urge, insulting and cruel.

Yet, try as she might, she could not escape from the bonds of her own response. Her mouth bit at his and he laughed beneath his breath and returned her bites, nibbling at the sensitive skin of her lips until the fever in her blood burnt away all inhibitions.

She whimpered, savaged by a smouldering in her loins, an inescapable need for something unknown.

'What is it?' he asked. 'What do you want, Lora?'

That first burning kiss had pressed her head back into his shoulder, exposing the pale, vulnerable length of her throat. Shudders began to build as she responded to the heat of his mouth there, stopping the breath behind the kisses.

She moaned, a long sigh of renunciation and fear, and whispered his name. Perhaps it was a signal he had been waiting for.

His hands, which had been so cruelly tight on her unwilling body, relaxed, smoothed the burning skin in a movement at once soothing and inflammatory. She turned her head fretfully and his mouth found the hollow at the base of her throat where a little traitorous pulse thudded a metronome of passion and need.

Dry-mouthed, a prisoner of sensation, she pressed her lips to the high cheekbone which was all that she could reach. Her tongue slid tentatively out, touched for a second the hot skin. She had never known that all her life she had wanted to know that particular taste, that it was sweet as honey, as necessary as salt, as exciting as a roller-coaster ride.

'Yes,' he said as, emboldened by the swift shudder her mouth had aroused, she turned towards his ear.

She had no idea what persuaded her, but when the darting stab of her tongue reached into the hidden spiral she felt his response to the little caress run like a shudder through his strong body, and was seized by a sensation of power unlike anything she had ever known. In her dazed state she thought that until this moment she had never known the exultation of her own will; all she had done until then was react to what others had done or said.

But now, with this man, she was a partner in what was happening; subordinate no longer, she had become an equal who was able to make him as witless and unrestrained as she was.

Then his hand slid up to her breast as he turned his head blindly into the softness and began to suckle.

Lora gasped, surrendering without a struggle to the piercing rapture of the moment. His hand shaped her flesh with the unerring possessiveness of experience, moulding it for the heated moisture of his mouth, turning her so that he could make each hard, tight bud his, and she shook and trembled in the throes of an excitement which became almost unbearable as it went on.

At last he lifted his head, heat along his cheekbones, the hard impersonality of lust fading a little as her blind pleasure registered.

'Oh, Lora,' he said huskily, 'why are you fighting this? I want you so much, and you—surely you can't deny this?'

She winced, the potent gratification fading a little so that the cool reason of her mind could surface. One hand crept from the tawny hair where it had been buried—holding him close, she realised with a shock of self-hatred—to cover a heart that was thudding with far more ecstasy than fear.

Through numb lips she said, 'No!' And a little more strongly, 'No—I can't!'

The demanding passion which carved his features darkened into something else. 'Come, now,' he sneered, 'it's too late for protestations of rectitude, Lora. I knew right from the start that you wanted me, and now you know it too.'

She stiffened, trying to pull herself free, but the embrace which had been paradise such a short time before was now a prison, holding her in fetters of iron.

'You're a tease,' he said, watching the play of emotions on her face as very deliberately he slid his hand from her chin down the length of her throat and on over her chest, to come to rest just above the neckline of her nightgown. The long, tanned fingers lay casually on her white skin, so strong, so, she reminded herself as she tore her eyes away from them to stare defiantly at him, so accustomed to this sort of dalliance.

But he was looking at them too, his face impassive until he lifted his head and fixed her with an inexorable stare. 'Look,' he said silkily. 'See how much you want me, Lora. See how useless it is to lie to me or to yourself. Your body knows.'

She knew what he had seen. Made transparent by the avid movements of his mouth, the white material of her nightgown revealed the nipples he had cherished, dark rose traitors.

She was exposed, her secrets open to him. It was useless to deny that she had wanted him—still wanted him, for she recognised the frustration which was aching through her body, crabbing inside her bones, impelling her towards a consummation, a satisfaction she did not know.

Laughing sardonically, he used his great strength to pull her closer, and laughed again when she flinched away from the evidence of his arousal.

'Neither of us can hide,' he said, with a curious satisfaction.

Anger and a burning humiliation gave her the strength to twist free; or perhaps he let her go, because he was smiling as she almost fell off his lap to stand, still held captive by his fingers around her elbow, beside the chair.

It occurred to her that he hadn't once stood up during this whole incident. For a man with Matt's bone-deep courtesy, that had to prove something! And wasn't standing supposed to give the stander some sensation of control?

Fat hope; it was the man lounging in the chair like a great cat, totally relaxed and at ease, who was totally in control. She felt as though she had been crushed by one of the great whales they had worked so hard to save.

A savage laughter was irradiating the golden eyes as he looked up at her, but it was the complacency behind the amusement that enraged her. Forgetting completely that she was standing barefoot in a nightgown which bore evidence of the moments when she had almost fainted in a sensual ecstasy, she lifted her chin with an odd little jerk and said in a voice she strove to make as cold and empty as possible, 'I'm going home tomorrow. And if you object, I'll tell them that you sexually harassed me.'

'You'd probably be able to convince them,' he agreed. He waited until she was almost trembling with a heady combination of anger and suspense, then said idly, 'It will be a damned nuisance if you flounce off to Auckland now. Shall we make a deal?'

'I told you what I thought of your deal,' she retorted, hiding her disappointment with aggression.

He smiled and said with soft cynicism, 'Ah, but this is a different deal. There's a lot of work arising from the field day, work that you'll be able to do with very little supervision. I don't want to have to drop everything to find a new secretary; from now until Christmas is my busiest time, and I'll be too occupied to break in someone else. I'd rather wait until after Christmas. If you stay until then, I'll call off my vendetta against your brother.'

CHAPTER SEVEN

LORA stared at him, her mind tumbling through a whirl of reactions, the main one being disappointment. She didn't ask herself the reason for this, but said huskily, 'You'll let Sandy come back? And work here?'

He inclined his head, his face totally without expression.

Lora heard her heart beat several times before she said carefully, 'You said I was wrong for assuming that you hounded him.' She searched his face for some hint of emotion, but there was nothing, no anger, no sign of the passion which only a few moments ago had darkened the golden skin. Just a hard look of indifference.

Uncertainly, she quoted his own words at him. What kind of man do you think I am? he had snarled, and she was horrified to discover just how much she wanted to believe him.

Still no response. His face remained impassive, calmly remote, the strong, handsome features composed; he had gone to some place where she couldn't reach him. He was awesomely self-sufficient, and he was using it as a weapon against her.

Angered by his control when she was having such difficulty with her emotions, she cried, 'If all that righteous indignation was genuine, if I have misjudged you, I don't need to stay.'

She had struck home somehow. The muscle beside his mouth flicked once, twice, but the look he directed at her was impersonal, coolly deliberate. 'You will have to decide whether you believe me.'

Lora glared at him with resentment and frustration, her mouth firming into a hard line. Afterwards she was never to know why she made the decision, except that his arrogance probably had a lot to do with it.

'In that case, I'll stay,' she said mutinously.

He smiled unpleasantly and got to his feet in a lithe movement which gave the lie to the intense effort he had exerted throughout the day. 'I wonder,' he murmured as he came towards her, 'whether you really want to disbelieve me, or whether you want to stay and see just what we do to each other.'

Her teeth clenched a painful moment on her lip. Casting him a look of sheer dislike, she said shortly, 'If you touch me again, I'll go. I mean it...'

But he laughed and bent his head, and she couldn't move, her whole body poised in sharp anticipation, singing and stirring because he was standing close to her. Lashes weighted and heavy with surrender, only her will kept her eyes open as she waited for the kiss.

It was not the searing embrace she had come to expect from him. His mouth was as light as a moth's wing, as the feather on a swallow, and he kissed her not on her expectant, eager mouth, but tenderly on her eyelids, closing her eyes one after the other. 'You must be exhausted,' he murmured. 'Saving whales all day, then so much unbridled emotion into the night. Go back to bed, Lora.'

The unhurried amusement in his voice was liberally laced with satisfaction; Lora's eyes flew open, then narrowed in an intense, unsmiling survey that transformed them into slivers of ice, pale as the polar seas and every bit as unyielding.

She had been manipulated and she knew it, and from the mockery in his face he knew she knew it and he thought it was funny!

Sheer animal rage fountained up through her body, the cold anger of the previous moment evaporating in an incandescent surge of emotion. Her hand clenched, then swung; with all of the power of her not inconsiderable strength, she hit him in the solar plexus.

He should have sagged, gasping, but he had seen what she was about to do and had an infinitesimal second to brace himself so that her fist met a sheet of muscle ready for the blow.

It hurt. She bit off a gasp of pain, then the realisation hit her, the enormity of what she had done, and she went white, her face a mask of anguished terror.

Matt had been smiling, his expression taut and threatening, but when she gave a low, broken cry and turned away the feral danger vanished from his face and he caught her shoulder, pulling her around so that he could see her.

'What is it?' She couldn't speak, and he shook her. 'Lora, what have I done?'

'Not you,' she whispered. 'Me.'

Her hands were pressed over her eyes. She saw her father in front of her, the fury in him so potent that it darkened the air, and for the first time in her life she thought she understood what drove him to such excesses of behaviour.

Matt's hand fell away from her skin as though he couldn't bear to touch her. He said in a voice that strove to be steady, 'You hit me. It didn't hurt and it served me right. I wanted to make you angry. I asked for it.'

'Nobody asks to be hit.'

The words echoed starkly in the quiet room. She was trembling, fine shivers pulling at her skin as she tried to assimilate the truth. She was like her father.

And she had always known it. She had lied to herself, told herself that she had never fallen in love, never met a man who attracted her, even that she was afraid of men; but deep inside she had known that she dared not let herself love, because she had it in her to kill the one she loved.

She had not thought it necessary to armour herself against Matt. Oh, she had recognised the attraction, but in her blind vanity she had thought she could deal with that, that she would never fall in love with a man who had done to Sandy what Matt had done.

And so her love had been seeded in darkness, nurtured in secrecy and flowered without her being aware of it.

But she knew now that she loved him, and knew that, like her father, she was in the grip of an obsession which could only lead to degradation.

'Lora,' he said when it became obvious that she wasn't going to speak. 'Were you abused—beaten—when you were a child?'

His perception shocked her out of the stasis of despair. Colour flooded her cheeks and she turned her head away, allowing it to sink low so that he couldn't see the shame and embarrassment written so large in her face. Her first instinct was to lie. In fact, the negative was hovering on her lips, but she couldn't pronounce it.

Instead she summoned the strength to say in a reasonably level tone, 'I'm sorry I lost my temper. It won't happen again——'

'Don't,' he said between his teeth, 'think you can put me off with that polite, aloof little voice. I'm going to find out why you behave the way you do if I have to smash down every one of the barriers you've erected around your cowering little soul. Were you beaten?'

Terrified by the ruthless determination she saw in him, she snatched her gaze away as though he burnt her eyes, and said hopelessly, 'Yes.'

His expression set into lines of pure fury. After a short struggle he was able to tamp down the emotions in his face, except for the molten ferocity in his eyes. 'By whom?'

Her lips were dry, almost painful, but she had no moisture in her mouth to ease them. 'My father,' she said in a hurried whisper.

'He beat you?'

'No—well, not often. Sometimes. He beat Sandy more.'

His expression altered, set into lines of icy control, except for the glittering fire beneath his lashes. 'What did he do? How did he abuse you?'

It was too much; she couldn't tell him, not now when she had only just realised that the demons driving her father lurked in her, waiting only for strong emotion to release them. She pulled away, turning in on herself, fighting his concern the only way she knew how, by withdrawing. 'More mental and emotional,' she said calmly, her voice toneless, very cool and even.

'Sexually?'

Then she understood the immense reluctance in his voice as well as the searing anger. 'Oh, no,' she whispered, appalled. 'No. He loved my mother. He—never...'

'He used to grab you by the wrists.' His voice too was level, almost without inflection.

She couldn't prevent the startled glance. He smiled, a wolfish, frightening movement of his lips, and said, 'You reacted to the way I touched you there with something like terrified desperation. I was angry with myself because I'd lost control and hurt you, not my usual method of dealing with recalcitrant women, but I thought there was more to it than pain and disgust.'

Yes, she remembered the incident. The second night she had spent at Kahurangi. She was astounded that he had, though.

She managed a casual shrug. 'It doesn't matter. I have this thing about being touched, but it's my problem.'

He didn't like her dismissive tone, or the words. She sensed the sudden tension in him, saw the way his eyes narrowed into slits of molten gold, and found herself wondering if she had overdone it.

Silkily he said, 'Not always,' and watched with hard interest as the colour drained from her skin and she made a little gesture with her hand as though warding him off.

But when she faced him it was to see him scanning the white contours of her face.

'You're tired,' he said unexpectedly. 'We'll talk about this when you've had a night's sleep. Go up to bed.'

Relief flooded her, and on its heels came exhaustion, black and heavy. She wavered a little, but no self-possessed way of saying goodnight came to her mind, so she turned and went over to the door.

He let her get as far as the door before saying quietly, 'Lora, you're going to tell me exactly what happened.'

'You have no right——'

He interrupted with harsh emphasis. 'You may not accept it yet, but you have given me the right. And one day you are going to accept that not all men are like your father. He was sick.'

She almost told him then. She couldn't bear him to assume that she was afraid of him, that she thought he would hurt her as her father hurt her mother. But the words were ashes in her mouth, for if she did that she would have to admit that she was the one who suffered from the illness, she the one who was flawed.

And she could not do it. More than anything else, she wanted him to think well of her.

She did not sleep that night. All of the long hours she sat by the window and stared out through the branches of the jacaranda, still leafless but hazed with the bright blue-purple of the buds. Within a week it would be brilliant, a joyous welcome to the summer. She watched as the stars glittered like promises through the branches, huddled still in her chair when the sky was darkened by cloud and heard the first heavy downpour without emotion.

Some time in the small hours the light in Matt's room bloomed briefly, then was dark. Was he sleeping, or was he lying wakeful, wondering how he could overcome what he saw as the chief obstacle to—to what?

He had said nothing about love.

She shrank back into the chair, her heart a small knot of pain in her breast. His words echoed coldly in her ears. 'We're dynamite together.' That did not sound like love. Lust, she thought bitterly, and tried to persuade herself that the tenderness she had seen in his eyes, heard in his voice, had only been a means to an end.

She remembered a photograph she had seen of Amber Stephanides, small and voluptuous, her beauty blazing through the grainy newspaper black and white. Lora's eyes closed in pain. What hope had she? Amber—even her name spoke of warmth.

But Lora was tall and coldly pale and fatally flawed. Even if he loved her as much as she did him, she would never allow herself to take what fate offered so temptingly. If she hesitated, she had only to think of her mother's life—and the bitter sickness that drove her father to cage the woman he loved in a prison forged of love's bars.

Strange, she thought wearily as a sullen, wet dawn broke over the sea, that it should take her until now to see that her father was as much a prisoner in that cage as her mother.

She knew that she looked washed out, her skin sallow and the circles blue under her eyes, but she made herself go down to breakfast. It didn't help that Matt looked as though he had slept peacefully all night, or that when she looked at him she felt a curious breaking sensation in her chest and all common sense fled into a limbo of remembered sensuality.

'That's better,' he said, watching the colour heat her skin. 'You look as though you had a bad night.'

He didn't seem sympathetic, so she remained obstinately silent, merely shooting a speaking glance his way before concentrating on her coffee.

Not in the least intimidated, he went on, 'I've had a call from Auckland. Unfortunately, it's not something I can deal with from here, so I'll have to go down today. I doubt if I can finish the business by tonight. Can I trust you not to leave while I'm away?'

Coldly she returned, 'I told you I'd stay if you promised to stop hounding Sandy.'

He laughed softly. 'So you did. Regretting it now?'

This brought her head up. 'No.'

'Of course you are.' An ironic little smile hardened the line of his mouth as he added enigmatically, 'I've always been a gambler.'

'Reckless,' she said with delicate scorn.

He grinned. 'You've been listening to Jane. Now, the only thing that's essential while I'm away is the wages. However, there's plenty of tidying up on the files to do. I've left instructions—if you want any clarification, let me know before I leave.'

'How long will you be away?'

He lifted a brow at her, at once quizzical and teasing. 'Three days. Are you going to let yourself miss me?'

'That depends on how much work you've left for me.'

He laughed and got to his feet, bending over the table to drop a kiss on her bent bright head. 'Enough to keep you from getting bored. I've left the phone number in case you need to contact me for any reason. Lora?'

Unwillingly she lifted her head to look at him. He was scanning her face almost hungrily, she thought, surprised.

'Don't worry,' he said, and she was disarmed again by that unexpected tenderness. 'We'll work it out.'

He left an hour later, and when Lora went into the kitchen for her morning tea it was to find Meri, Moana on her hip, commiserating with Jane because the weather was so foul.

'The forecasters have been saying that it's because of El Niño,' Meri said cheerfully. 'Although how the weather off South America can affect us here, I'm darned if I know! Our weather patterns go from west to east, not vice versa.'

Jane poured the tea and sat down. 'Don't ask me. I thought it was the Southern Oscillation, and no, I have no idea what that means, except that it brings drought and wind and nasty weather.'

Lora found that they were both looking expectantly at her. When she hastily disclaimed any further knowledge on the matter, the subject was dropped. Although Jane did say, 'I hate it when Matt flies in weather like this. And the house always seems empty until he comes back.'

She was right. The house seemed more than empty, it was desolate. Lora kept her head down and worked harder than she had ever done before, so that the hours flew and the time when Matt came back came closer and closer. After a couple of days of heavy rain the weather cleared; Jane shooed her out of the house.

'You've been working like a stevedore,' she said. 'You look definitely fragile around the eyes. Why don't you take this bag of wool I've spun down to Meri? And while you're there, see if you can coax her out, too. She must be exhausted, shut up in the house with the children these past days.'

Meri did look tired, even though her husband had taken Peter out with him for the afternoon. She welcomed the suggestion of a walk with delight.

'The kids aren't naughty,' she said as she dressed Moana in her bright red raincoat and tiny matching gumboots, 'but they don't like being cooped up for days on end, and they fight. I've been trying to get a length of weaving done, but no chance.'

Once outside they looked around, trying to decide whether to go up to the Angora goats and be beguiled by the antics of the kids, or walk in the other direction.

'Horsies,' Moana said firmly, making up their minds for them.

Both women laughed and followed the determined little figure.

'Two kids who are crazy about horses!' Meri groaned. 'I have to keep the gate locked and watch her like a hawk, otherwise she's out of the garden and across the paddock. Matt's brought her back a couple of times, perched up in front of him. And I'm sure that only encourages her.

She loves riding with him. All the confidence in the world!'

The race had enough puddles in it to provide joy and rapture for Moana, but in spite of the delights of stamping and splashing she headed steadily for the horse paddock. Once there, she chattered and called to the curious animals, most of whom came up to renew acquaintance with her, blowing delicately into the tiny starfish hands.

Watching the way Meri laughed with her daughter, the warmth and complete trust shown by the child as she perched on her mother's hip, Lora felt an ache deep in her chest, one she immediately repressed. It was useless to dream . . . but for a few seconds that was what she did, imagining Matt's child in her arms, strong and sturdy and golden . . .

'That must be the waterfall,' Meri said, breaking into Lora's thoughts. 'Shall we go and see it? Then Moana and I must get back; it looks as though there might be more rain on the way.'

The bridge above the fall was only just above the level of the water that surged by, thick and pale clay in colour; a spate that gave no indication of the sight that awaited them, although the deep thunder of the waters hinted at it.

Once there, they stood in awe. The wind from the north had brought warm rain in constant heavy showers, and the sheet of volcanic rock that formed the falls was covered by the flow of water, discoloured and frothing as it shot out over the lip and smashed down on to the rocks at the base. On either side the trees grew down the cliff in all shades of vivid green, the soaked leaves hanging low and sullen.

Lora watched its hypnotic flow for a time, then turned as Moana cried out. Secure in her mother's arms, she was wriggling and pointing to something in the paddock below. Above the roar of the waters Lora heard her call, 'Horsey! Look!'

Sure enough, there was the horse, and there, beside her, a foal.

Meri gave her daughter a hunted look. 'Eyes like an eagle's,' she said loudly above the noise. 'She can pick up a horse at a couple of miles. Especially foals. No, darling, we are not going down to look at Delight's baby, not today. Look at that big black cloud over there, coming our way. If we don't get back home, my treasure, it's going to rain all over us, and then we'll be wet as puppydogs. Come on, let's gallop off home.'

Talking cheerfully, she overrode Moana's wail of protest, and with Lora as a willing accessory galloped all the way back to the house.

Sure enough, almost the moment she arrived back at the homestead it began to rain again, but it seemed that that was the last effort of the depression, for there was none from then until Lora went to bed. And as she lay looking out through her window, expectant and excited because Matt was coming home tomorrow, it was to see stars through the branches.

But first she had to get through the morning. It was going to be slow, because she had finished everything he had left for her to do, as well as quite a bit of work she had done on her own initiative, and although the sun was smiling beneficently over the sodden countryside and the colours were glowing and the earth smelt of summer, she had to wait out the cold, lonely hours until the late afternoon when he was due home.

Keren solved part of the problem by turning up shortly before morning tea, armed with flowers and a beautifully wrapped parcel.

'Matt likes the way I do flowers,' she informed a stiffly disapproving Jane, 'so I'm going to put a bowl in his bedroom.' She flashed a taunting, complacent look at Lora as she emerged from the office. 'See, I've brought roses exactly the right shade to go with his curtains and bedspread. And a welcome-home gift for him, too.'

The flowers were glowing in exquisite shades of apricot and gold and buff, and their scent was heavenly. Lora mastered the fierce pang of jealousy that ripped through her composure and waited while Jane said woodenly, 'Very well. If you'll come through to the garden room you can do them there. I'll see that they get up to his room.'

Tight-lipped and inexorable, she led a mutinous but silent Keren through to the room at the back of the house where all of the paraphernalia involved in flower-arranging was kept, then came back into the kitchen.

'I'll bring you your tea,' she said.

Startled, because she had got into the habit of having both morning and afternoon tea with the housekeeper, Lora allowed herself to be ushered out on to the terrace where she and Matt had sat the first morning she had spent at Kahurangi. A little hurt, she wondered whether the relaxation she had noticed in the older woman's attitude had only been temporary.

Jane disabused her of this. 'Little madam,' she said beneath her breath as she brought the tray through. 'I'm not having her in my kitchen acting as though she owns it.'

Lora said nothing, and Jane gave her a wry smile. 'She rubs me up the wrong way,' she said unnecessarily. 'When she came back from that job in Auckland she made a dead set at young Tim, and then dropped him like a hot cake when she thought she had a chance with Matt. He was only being kind to her, but she might have hurt Tim badly, and she couldn't care less. The Smitherses have ruined her.'

She had no time to say anything more, for a clack of heels announced Keren's arrival on to the terrace. Dressed in a short skirt that showed off her good legs, she looked young and vibrant with life—everything that Lora was not, she thought despondently.

'Oh, lovely.' Keren looked immensely pleased with herself. 'Thank you, Jane. I'll pour.'

Jane left, her erect back expressive of her outrage, and Keren smiled confidently across the table as she wielded teapot and the milk-jug. 'You must be just about ready to go back to Auckland,' she purred.

Lora's brows lifted, but the expectant look in the younger woman's eyes stilled her reply. She contented herself with a non-committal nod and tried not to notice the angry glitter it caused.

But Keren persevered. 'After all, you've done all that you were employed to do, haven't you?'

'I believe so.' Lora's tone was cool and polite.

'Of course, I understand if you want to stay. I don't suppose you've ever been in such nice surroundings before.' She glanced around as though Kahurangi and its beauty were all her doing.

Lora thought of some of the places she had worked in, the palatial hotels and millionaires' penthouses, and hid a smile. But in a way Keren was right. No other place she had ever seen had the homestead's gracious elegance and comfort. 'It's certainly lovely here,' she agreed mildly.

'Naturally you want to stay as long as you can. Especially as, like every woman in the district, you've rather fallen for your employer! But Matt can be very cruel to silly women who make nuisances of themselves over him.' Keren was a little needled by Lora's lack of response, and she almost hissed the last sentence.

Lora said evenly, 'I believe you've already told me that.'

'But you haven't taken any notice. You're still here.'

'As you pointed out, it's Matt who employs me, and it will be Matt who tells me when to go, not the niece of a neighbour,' Lora said with cool courtesy.

All appearance of calm reason evaporated. The satin skin mottled in a manner both ugly and revealing as Keren spluttered, 'How dare you speak to me like that? Who do you think you are? Matt——'

'I am sure that Matt would agree with me on the impropriety of anyone but my employer's sending me back to Auckland,' Lora drawled, angry herself now, assailed by a flash of the bitter possessiveness she dreaded. She salvaged a degree of control by picking up her cup of tea and drinking, then set it down again when Keren flounced to the attack again.

'I'm going to tell him that you were rude to me,' she threatened.

'Just as you told him that you had eavesdropped on a conversation I had with my boss.' Lora's voice was cold and scornful, the words flicked with a whiplash strength.

Keren gasped, but rallied. 'I didn't—I overheard—I couldn't help hearing what you were saying. And then I had to tell Matt you are Sandy What's-his-name's sister,' she spat. 'He had a right to know. After all, Sandy only cost him thousands of dollars by selling secrets! You could be planning to do exactly the same. Matt had to know. I thought it was very suspicious you hadn't told him that that man was your brother.'

Lora looked at her, ignoring every vicious comment but the most important. 'Sandy,' she said in a voice flat with deliberation, 'did not sell secrets to anyone.'

Keren laughed unpleasantly. 'If he didn't, he was altogether too stupid. Surely he didn't just *give* them away to another stupid woman who thought because Matt took her to bed she had some sort of claim on him.' A hateful sophistication sharpened the clear voice. 'Men like Matt don't work that way. He'll enjoy any woman he wants, but when he marries it will be someone who won't shame him in front of his friends, someone who knows how to behave. Someone from his own level of society. Not a jumped-up little tart with only her looks to recommend her.'

Lora looked at her thoughtfully, saddened and repelled by her cynical and totally false view of the man she clearly hoped to marry. 'Possibly,' she murmured non-committally. 'But as it's not going to affect me, I don't see that we need to have this conversation.'

Keren looked at her still full cup of tea, then scrambled suddenly to her feet. 'I'm not going to bandy words with you,' she said in a lofty, immeasurably superior tone. 'Just remember that you are nothing—a nobody!—and keep out of my way in future.'

Feeling slightly sick, Lora watched her sway into the house, to be almost immediately replaced by an indignant Jane, who made no attempt to hide the fact that she had heard at least the last part of the exchange.

'Nosy little brat. The cheek of her!' she muttered, snatching the tea things on to the tray. 'She wouldn't dare carry on like that if Matt were home; he'd soon give her the runaround! Thinks just because her uncle is a friend of Matt's that she can do what she likes here, but she's too scared of his temper to try it in front of him!'

Lora made soothing noises, and waited until she had gone before turning her attention to the garden. The rain had brought the flowers and shrubs to full glory, and although the cherry was finished the last flowers still lingered on the magnolia branches. The scent of jasmine floated on the air, the fragile flowers surprisingly unmarked by the weather. Slowly the sweet promise and peace eased Lora's mind.

Yet the nagging little question remained. Oh, she could discount Keren's cynical view of Matt's character, but perhaps he chose women he could not love for another reason. Perhaps he had loved Amber Stephanides too much for any woman to take her place.

She found herself wondering if this was true when she drove into Paihia. It hurt, the prospect of Matt hurting; a wry smile twisted her generous mouth as she picked up some registered mail from the post office. Oh, she had read enough about love, and secretly believed none of it, but now she knew that, when you loved, the welfare of the loved one became paramount. If it would save Matt any pain at all, she would welcome it into her life.

It wasn't until later that she realised that she didn't feel that terrifying, searing jealousy whenever she thought of Amber. Just a kind of weary resignation, because who was she even to wonder if she might be able to compete with the other woman?

The road back claimed her full concentration; it was rutted and dangerous in parts where the heavy rain had washed the gravel into the ditches. She pushed all thoughts of Matt and his women and his imminent arrival to the back of her mind, frowning slightly as her eyes were caught by the streak of yellow-white that was the waterfall. Normally the lazy little stream was impossible to pick out through the screen of trees that hid it from the road, but in full spate it captured her attention. There was, she thought, something different—ah, yes, on one side the thin layer of earth over the rocks had slipped away, carrying trees and undergrowth with it, and leaving an ugly scar.

A pity, but, if that was all the damage the downpour had done, they had got off lightly. There had been floods further south. And the rain would set the countryside up for the summer. No drought this year, if all went well.

Back at the station she found herself prowling restlessly, willing away the hours until she could go to airport to pick up Matt. It was humiliating to be so dependent on a man... She tried to whip up resentment, but all she could feel was that deep, wild, unbidden excitement. A quick glance in the mirror revealed a darkening of her pale eyes so that they gleamed with a febrile light, and there was a wildfire flush accentuating the high sweep of her cheekbones.

Even her mouth looked different, she thought despairingly. Oh, it was the same shape, the same texture, but there was a new softness, a blatant sensuality that had never been there before. Was this what Keren had noticed? The reason for that nasty little incident over the teatray?

The telephone interrupted her reverie. With a resigned little shrug she picked up the receiver. It was Matt ringing from the tiny airport at Kerikeri.

At the sound of his voice Lora's blood ran through her veins in a sweep of honey, slow as the tides of life, fast as lightning, a mingling of wildfire and pain. 'Yes,' she said, her voice cool and quiet. 'I'll be there in ten minutes.'

Behind her the telephone rang again, but she left it, walking with free, unfettered grace out to the car.

He was waiting, leaning with casual male elegance against the wall, ignoring the rapt attention of several tourists. Lora's eyes caressed him as she walked towards him; he was, she thought exultantly, perfect, her golden man, all lithe power and magnetism. The bright northern sun lingered lovingly on his tawny hair, picked out the splendid male sculpturing of feature and structure, the slightly hooked nose, the slashing strength of jaw and cheekbone, the sensual twist of the firm mouth.

As she came up to him he straightened up and smiled, and she realised that he had been watching her too; there was a wry sympathy in the amber depths of his eyes, barely overlaying a steady glow that fired their depths into licks of flame.

'Hello,' he said, and took her totally by surprise by bending his head and kissing her cheek.

It was not a passionate embrace; Matt was not one who paraded his emotions for public delectation, but his lips were warm and they lingered just long enough to bring the heat up through her clear skin.

She looked up into his face, her eyes for once unguarded, and caught her breath. 'Hello,' she said huskily.

She knew what he saw in her face and she did not blame him for the satisfaction she could read in his; all of her fears seemed faded and unimportant, logic and reason reduced only to the basic fact of her love for him.

So she smiled, and didn't even try to stop her lips from trembling.

'Let's go home.' As he bent to pick up his briefcase and the overnight bag, she caught a flash of envy in the expression of the other women.

'I'll take the briefcase,' she said, scarcely knowing what the words were.

He laughed softly. 'No need. It's not too heavy.'

He put her into the driver's seat and sat himself on the other side with a little unconscious grunt of pleasure that revealed how tired he was. Once out on the road he said, 'I like watching you drive. Your forehead creases in a most distracting way. Have you finally given in, Lora?'

Just for a moment her lip was caught between her teeth, but almost immediately she relaxed and said simply, 'Yes.'

'So you'll allow me to court you?'

A kind of rapturous uncertainty kept her eyes fixed on to the road. 'I—is that what you want to do?'

'No.' But before she had time to feel more than a crushing weight of disappointment he laughed harshly and said, 'Oh, no, I'm as impatient as any man. I want to take you to bed, tonight if not sooner, but I can wait. You have to learn that you can trust me, that I'll never abuse your trust as your father did. So I'll wait, and woo you, because when you come to me I want it to be perfect for you.'

No word of love, but she had not expected one. And when she cast a sideways look at him she saw the lines of tension across his forehead. In a voice she didn't recognise, she said huskily. 'It will be...tonight.'

Without looking at him, she recognised his stillness. 'Are you sure? Is this a complete surrender, Lora?'

'Yes.' Her voice shook a little. 'I missed you.'

He exhaled a long breath. 'Yes,' he said slowly. 'As if I'd lost a vital part of me. Lying awake, remembering how you looked that last night—so beautiful and wild, with your eyes glazed and drowsy—I swear I could almost feel the warm smoothness of your skin. Such innocent abandon—and such exciting spirit.'

Colour heated her skin again. As she swung off the main road on to the gravel, she said, 'I should have run like hell away from here the minute I saw you.'

In an entirely different voice, he said, 'What the hell—Lora, what's happened? Why are the men walking across the horse paddock?'

'I don't know.' Gravel spurted from the wheels as she put her foot down hard on the accelerator. 'They can't be—but they look as though they're searching for something.'

CHAPTER EIGHT

Two strange cars were parked outside the homestead, and even as Lora switched off the key Jane came out, almost running, her face pale.

Matt was half-way to meet her by the time Lora swung her long legs free of the car. He said urgently, 'What's happened?'

'Thank heaven you're here! It's little Moana. She's been missing for the last hour—Meri's been looking for her but there's no sign of her. I've sent out all the men——'

Matt swung around as Lora said on a note of dread, 'Oh, no...'

What followed was a blur of activity. Within ten minutes the police had been notified and the search co-ordinated. Matt moved with slashing speed, and was gone to oversee the search when the police car arrived.

The constable listened to Lora's recapitulation of the sequence of events, then promised calmly, 'We'll find her; she's too small to have wandered far. If no one saw her, she's almost certain to be close to home.'

'Jane said that none of the workers caught so much as a glimpse of her.'

'They searched her parents' house?'

Lora nodded. Matt had asked the same question. 'Yes. Then they spread out from the house.'

The policeman gave a satisfied nod. 'You'd be surprised the number of times they creep under a bed or into a cupboard and go to sleep. Will you come down to the parents' house with me? I want to speak to her mother, get some details of what she was wearing, that sort of thing. And what exactly happened. Then I can

decide whether to call for volunteers to help in th
search.'

After the first frantic minutes spent looking on he
own, Meri had been prevailed upon to wait at home i
case the little girl wandered back. Lora nodded, her hear
aching. 'I'll just tell the housekeeper here,' she said.

Jane was baking, whipping up a batch of scones. He
busy hands didn't still while Lora told her where she wa
going, rolling out the dough as though her sanity de
pended on it.

'If they call for volunteers, we're going to need these,
she said, following Lora's gaze. 'Yes, you go ahead. I'l
join you as soon as I've finished here. Stay with her
Lora. She needs someone.'

The strain was only too evident on Meri's face: he
brown eyes, normally snapping and alert, were shadowec
by an intolerable tension; great dark circles had ap
peared beneath them and her mouth was taut with pain
Peter clung to her, his round little face worried anc
frightened. However, she spoke without any hesitatior
or tremor, succinctly giving the policeman the infor
mation he needed.

At last the constable said gently, 'Thank you, that'
all. If there's anything you remember, any little clue tha
might tell us where she was headed, let me know.'

Meri waited until he had left the room before whis
pering, 'I can't remember anything... Oh, Lora, there'
miles of coastline—and all the creeks and troughs...'

Lora could say nothing, but her face spoke for her,
and the quick involuntary pressure of her arms as sh
hugged Meri.

'What can I do?' she asked. 'Are you alone here?'

Meri shook her head, then her face crumpled and sh
nodded. 'The others wanted to come but I wouldn't le
them,' she said wearily. 'I wanted to think, to concen
trate, in case Moana said anything, gave me some sor
of hint that might help, but all I can do is listen to m
thoughts chase round and round my brain. I was weaving

this morning—I wanted to get it finished and I didn't take much notice of her chattering. What if she said something and I didn't hear? Lora—she's so little, only a baby. What if they don't find her before it's dark?'

Lora said briskly, 'It's at least two hours before the sun goes down, and Meri, even if they don't find her before then, I've read that most small children who find themselves alone at night just curl up and go to sleep without any trauma at all. Don't worry about that.'

Meri hugged Peter to her as though he were a shield. Her lips trembled as she whispered, 'It stops me from worrying about worse things.'

Lora didn't know what to say, for those same hideous suppositions were racing through her brain too. To allay them, she said, 'I'm going to make you a cup of tea and get you something to eat. Has Pete had his dinner?'

'Yes. But I don't want anything to eat. It would make me sick.'

Lora knew better than to protest, but was relieved when a knock at the door heralded a woman she recognised as the wife of one of the shepherds. In her hand was a covered dish. She looked a little startled at seeing Lora there, but agreed with her that Meri needed food to keep her strength up.

Between them they managed to persuade Meri to eat a small amount and drink some tea; as she was finishing, the young policeman came back and told them he had called for volunteers to help search. After that, things became hectic.

The policeman's call for volunteers produced a steady trickle of people, including the local fire brigade and members of the rugby club. Although still informal, a kind of search headquarters was in the process of being set up, and before long women began to arrive, most, like Jane, bearing food.

A couple of Meri's close friends arrived and Lora relinquished her into their care and went to join the others. The kitchen seemed full of women, all busy, all wearing identical expressions of concern and a determination not to show the fear that lurks at the base of every mother's heart. Lora picked up a teatowel and started to dry the cups that Jane was washing.

A glance through the window revealed a golden landscape, serene and lovely in the rays of the west-moving sun. Moana had been missing for over two hours.

A few minutes later the sound of cars drawing up outside lifted a few heads, but the women went on working, cutting sandwiches, pouring tea, cutting slices of cakes and loaves that they had brought to help feed tired men when they began to filter back.

Lora worked desperately, trying to banish the images that hovered just behind her thoughts, of Moana lost and frightened and cold, images that were ominous and yet easier to bear than other, more sinister fears, unspoken, even repelled, yet always there.

'How many men are searching?' she asked Jane once, as the sound of an engine announced yet another vehicle.

'Just about everyone in the district,' was the terse reply. 'Quite a few tourists wanted to help, but the police have decided that for the present it's better if only the locals go out.'

Lora nodded; she poured a cup of coffee, and said quietly, 'I'll take this in to Meri.'

'Put a drop of brandy in it.'

Lora hesitated, then added about a teaspoonful. Meri was huddled in the rocking chair, a sleeping Peter in her arms. Her friends sat close by. She seemed to have shrunk and when she looked up Lora almost wept for her.

'Thanks,' she said wearily, gesturing at the small table beside the chair. Peter moved and cuddled in closer, his adorable little face flushed and serene in sleep.

Lora suggested, 'Shall I take him while you drink that coffee?'

'No!' The reply was fierce and instinctive, accompanied by a tightening of her arms. Peter stirred, murmuring sleepily, then settled down again. Meri looked into his face, and tears filled her eyes. 'Oh, Lora,' she whispered, 'I'm so frightened.'

Lora said calmly, 'Of course you are, but you know, don't you, that there are men searching practically every inch of this place? If it's at all possible, they'll find her.'

'Yes, I know. Oh, I know they'll do their best, but what if it isn't good enough?'

Slowly, afraid that whatever she said would add to Meri's pain, Lora said, 'I read somewhere that we are never given more than we can bear, Meri.'

One of the friends made an indignant noise, but although the tears came afresh to Meri's eyes she nodded. 'Thank you,' she whispered as she adjusted the child in her arms and reached out a hand for the cup of tea. She drank a little, grimacing as she tasted the brandy, but said nothing about it.

Back in the kitchen Lora said fiercely, 'Oh, if there were only something I could *do*!'

'You don't know the place well enough to go out and search.' As always, Jane was common sense personified, but it didn't help to know that she was right.

By ten o'clock the search had been called off for the night, but a sedated Meri was still refusing to go to bed in case Moana came back. With Pete still asleep in her lap, she sat clutching her husband's hand, and listening with burning, tearless eyes as he and Matt talked.

Sadly, Jane and Lora went out to the Land Rover to drive back to the homestead. Jane looked up into the sky where stars peeped coyly through elongated wisps of cloud.

'Still mares' tails,' she said. 'It will be hot tomorrow.'

The hair on the back of Lora's neck prickled. She breathed, 'Mares' tails?'

Into her mind there popped an image, sharp and clearcut as a miniature, of the mare with her foal. And Moana demanding to go down to see them. The green grass, the little girl's eager face above her red raincoat, and the roar of the falls in the background. Could she have set out to see Delight's foal? But surely they had searched down there?

She said uncertainly, 'I—I'd like to go to the falls.'

Jane sent her a sharp glance, but said merely, 'All right.'

The Land Rover smelt of wet dog and oilskins and failure; Lora muttered, 'I'll drive, you must be worn out.'

Jane settled into the passenger seat, saying flatly, 'This sort of thing certainly takes it out of you. Uncertainty is worse than anything. Not to know...'

Both women lapsed into silence, unable to suppress their gloomy thoughts but unwilling to give voice to them and thus allow them some credibility, until they came to the fork in the road which took them down towards the waterfall.

A Lora turned the wheel, Jane roused herself to say, 'Any reason for this?'

Not even to herself would Lora admit that she had been worrying over the strange little memory. 'No. I just need some air.'

Of course Jane wasn't fooled. Gently, for her, she said, 'They've searched all along here, Lora. And it's unlikely that she would have managed to get this far. She was only gone twenty minutes before Meri missed her.'

'I know, I know, it's stupid...'

'But you want to check it out.' Jane nodded. 'All right, I won't tell anyone!'

Lora smiled mirthlessly.

At the head of the falls she switched off the Land Rover's lights and with Jane walked across the springy grass towards the little creek which had, over who knew how many thousands of years, carved itself a slot into the face of the old lava-flow. Swollen by the rain, the compressed water surged out in a smoothly powerful jet.

'There's a slip half-way down the other side,' she told Jane, pitching her voice above the roar of the water. 'The big kowhai tree has gone. I saw it as I was coming home from Paihia.' She leaned against the fence and looked over. 'Oh, it looks as though even more has gone.'

'Where?' Jane leaned forward to look down and across at the scar where the earth had torn free, leaving the bedrock glistening in the light of the moon. 'Matt will be sorry. He loved that tree——'

Her voice altered so abruptly on the last word that Lora jumped, but before she could ask she too had seen what the housekeeper's probing gaze had found. A small heap of something on a ledge close to the pounding chute of water, flotsam left marooned by the slip. Probably it was a clump of reeds brought down by the flood, but it could also be a toddler, hurt and in peril.

Lora whirled, ran back to the Land Rover and whipped out the torch, praying that its beam would reach the sixty feet or so down. She was not conscious of thinking; indeed, all that echoed in her brain was the knowledge that if that little mound was Moana she dared not shine the torch on her face in case she woke her and the child fell off the narrow ledge which was both her refuge and her prison.

Not even in her own mind did Lora admit the possibility that she might be dead.

The torch beam crossed the smooth, treacherous fall of water, hesitated, probed, hesitating again; beside her she could hear Jane whispering something—perhaps a prayer. Slowly she inched the beam towards the ledge, until it illuminated a small red gumboot. It didn't move. Lora dared an infinitesimal probe further.

Jane made a jerky movement of her arm and muttered something. The cone of light swung, shuddered, then steadied. Moana was asleep or unconscious, huddled in a heap so close to the edge that it was a miracle she hadn't been swept to her death.

Switching the torch off, Lora drew in a jagged breath.

'Is she all right?' Jane's voice was hoarse.

'I think so. Oh, God, I hope so! She must have walked out and then been stranded when that part of the bank slipped away.' Lora spoke abstractedly, her brain eagerly seizing on plan after plan as she tried to work out what to do. After a tense few moments, she made up her mind. 'You take the Land Rover back and raise the alarm.'

'What will you do?'

'I'll go down to the bottom and climb up to her.'

'But Lora——'

'If—if she's just asleep, she might wake; someone is going to have to get to her. If she's frightened by what's happening, she's likely to go over the edge. I've done quite a bit of climbing with my brother. It won't take me long to get up there—in fact, I'll be with her by the time they get here. I don't know how we'll get her off that ledge, but she'll have to have someone with her.'

Before Jane could utter the protest hovering on her lips, Lora ran across the bridge and climbed through the fence. As she began making her way through the tangle of bush that grew beside the falls, she felt fear like a sick heaviness in the pit of her stomach, but she knew that she had to be beside the child before anyone woke her.

Fortunately it was a glorious night now, warm and still, fragrant with the scents of summer. There was no moon yet, but the stars cast enough light to see by; that was going to be important, she thought with grim humour, because she couldn't climb up with the torch in her teeth.

To keep her mind off what might be waiting for her on the ledge, Lora planned carefully the climb up from the base of the falls, memorising as she made her way down beside it exactly how the rock had weathered, the way the crevices and fissures ran across the surface.

As it happened, she didn't have to go right to the rockfall at the bottom. About twenty feet above it a ledge extended invitingly out, angling into and slightly up the face. If she made her way to the end of it and stretched, she should be able to get to a sort of open chimney. It would take her a little while to get up that, but she knew the technique. And from there it was only a few feet to the ledge.

It was not a difficult climb, not even at night. Not even for a woman with a fear of heights. She swung the torch beam carefully over those few feet, nodding abruptly as she noticed at least four good handholds.

Taking a deep breath, she started upwards at the oozing rock, slick where the slip had torn away. From below there was no sign of the small huddle that was Moana. Lora tied the torch to the belt of her jeans with her handkerchief and began to climb. Her fear was a taste in her mouth, a roaring in her head, but she moved carefully and steadily, ignoring both her emotions and the pain from her shoulders and hands as she squirmed her way up the shallow chimney.

It wasn't as bad as she had expected. There were plenty of handholds and her eyes had adjusted well to the night so she was able to see without too much effort, but she pushed herself to get there before anything had a chance to wake the toddler who slept above.

As it happened, she didn't quite make it in time. The noise of the waterfall drowned out the sound of any engines, but, in the last, trickiest part when she strained to reach the ledge, the top of the cliff was suddenly outlined by a glowing halo of light as a vehicle came to a stop by the bridge.

In spite of the spray from the waterfall she was hot, sweat dripping dangerously into her eyes so that she had to stop and brush it away with her free hand. She had grazed her fingers and the blood seeped messily out over her hand; the raw skin stung like blazes. Out of the corner of her eye she saw movement at the top of the falls, and knew with a glad certitude that Matt was there. His presence lifted her confidence so that she was able to heave herself up the final few feet and over the lip on to the wet, slippery, narrow outcropping of rock where Moana lay.

She didn't stir, and remained sleeping all through the tense moments when Lora eased on to the ledge until her back was pressed painfully against the wet, cold stone. Her breath hurt her chest and she had to make a conscious effort to stop gasping in case the child woke and became frightened.

Almost fearfully her eyes searched the still little form. There was a cut on the smooth forehead, from which the blood still oozed, but it was shallow. A delicate probe with shaking fingers revealed no sign of a fracture or compression, so it seemed Moana had been lucky; apart from the cut she was undamaged, although of course it would need an X-ray to make sure.

Her skin was cool, but not cold. Lora slid her hand beneath the damp T-shirt and rested it against the little chest, dread making her movements slow, but she was almost instantly reassured by the rise and fall of the ribcage.

A further gentle exploration showed that there were no broken bones. None that she could feel, anyway.

Whether Moana was asleep or unconscious Lora couldn't tell, but she knew that it would be dangerous to move her, so she contented herself with putting a hand on the fragile shoulder. More as a gesture of solidarity, she thought, unamused at the trite phrase, than any sort of anchorage. It would be dangerous to both of them if the child woke. Afraid and disorientated, she might well put them in far greater jeopardy.

Lora lifted her eyes from the black drop of emptiness where her feet dangled, only to have them drawn irresistibly towards the hypnotic flow of the water. She swallowed, brutally assailed by helplessness, then spoke sternly to herself and closed her eyes. A piece of the ledge, small but too close, broke off and disappeared into the dark abyss below, followed by two or three others. The slip had torn away the thin layer of earth and tree roots that held the rock-face intact; with the covering gone, every weak place was exposed and vulnerable.

Lora waited while her heart slowed and the sweat dried cold on her brow. Beneath her fingers the little chest rose and fell evenly, calming and reassuring her, until she made the mistake of opening her eyes.

Her stomach lurched and she gave a stifled whimper as vertigo gripped. Seizing control with a fierce hand, she stamped on her panic, forcing herself to recite the times table until the sick horror faded, and she was able to think more or less calmly.

'Matt,' she whispered beneath her breath. 'Matt,' saying his name like a talisman.

And when she heard his voice it was as though she had summoned him herself from the depths of her need and love.

'Lora! Wave if you can hear me.'

Joy flooded her heart. She lifted her hand and waved it at where she gauged him to be, standing on the rockpile at the base of the cliff, forty or so feet below.

'Right. Is she hurt? Wave once if she's hurt.'

She gave an emphatic wave.

There was a short silence, as though he were conferring with someone else, then, 'Right, hang on for a few minutes more and we'll have you off there.'

It seemed hours, but it was only a few minutes until she heard the deep thudding of the big tractor above the constant roar of the waters. As she had feared, the noise woke Moana. Lora tightened her grip as the child stirred, her breath catching in hard little sobs.

Soothingly, pitching her voice just above the thunder of the waters, she spoke into the tiny ear. 'It's all right, sweetheart, don't fret now, it's all right. Lora's here, you're safe and soon you'll see Mummy and Daddy.'

She didn't know whether Moana could hear, but the jerky little movements eased, although her lashes still twitched. It didn't look like normal sleep to Lora. Frowning, she risked moving her hand to touch the narrow forehead. It felt icy cold beneath her fingers, and Moana stirred again and gave a choked, sobbing little cry, her sweet triangular mouth twisting for a moment.

Lora froze, for another piece of rock, this time under one knee, crumbled away into the night, scraping down her leg as it went so that she had to jerk herself even further back against the wet rock behind. After a paralysed moment she unclenched her hand and reached for the child, holding her little T-shirt in a grip of iron.

And then the strong beam of a spotlight dipped and probed, was joined by another from the base of the cliff, and finally both coalesced on the ledge, imprisoning them in a cage of light.

The brilliant glare made her close her eyes, but of course she had to open them. Just in time, for Moana suddenly twisted, trying to cower away from the din and the light. The sudden movement almost took her off the ledge. Lora shouted something and snatched at her, and for a stark moment her balance of gravity was pitched out over the cliff; she flung herself and the child back, hearing even above the noise of the water and the tractor the sound her breath made in her chest, tearing painfully in and out in great gasps. Moana began to wail, but stopped thrashing about as she felt Lora's arms enclose her in a fierce embrace.

What followed had the vivid, scrappy consistency of a nightmare. First of all a small farm gate was lowered. It lurched down the cliff on the side away from the water, the rope at each corner holding it more or less flat. In the middle was a child's harness, securely held on by yet more cord. Lora realised with something very close to panic that she was going to have to put Moana on to the thing herself.

More alone than she had ever been in her life, her hands trembling, she had to work out how to strap the dazed and terrified child on to it. It was a nightmare, but at least Moana was still, although when she was at last tied on to the makeshift stretcher she wailed, seeming to wake up properly for the first time.

Lora spoke soothingly to her, even smiled, before lifting both thumbs in the air. Then she waited, heart in her mouth, while slowly, painfully, the small burden was winched up. If she had made a mistake with the fastenings—if Moana slipped free—she would never forgive herself.

'Lora.' That was Matt.

She waved.

'The ropes will be down in a few minutes. Hang on, my love.'

A few minutes later there was activity above; she heard what might have been a cheer, and she said a silent prayer of thanksgiving.

And looked down. And froze, overcome by the old panic. Snatches of long-past scenes flashed behind her eyes; she saw her father holding her out over the cliff, heard her mother's anguished pleas and knew a recurrence of that sickening fear.

The roar of the water dashing itself on to the rocks at the base of the falls joined the roar in her ears; a dank sweat of terror broke out over her skin. Her breath panted in through lips slack with fear. The white foam so far beneath drew her eyes in sinister fascination, pulling at her, luring her.

Slowly, painfully, she leaned back, forcing herself to breathe deeply in an effort to avoid the hyperventilation she knew could lead to unconsciousness and a fall. And on those unforgiving rocks she would be lucky to escape with broken bones. She didn't know when the ropes slithered down past her, she was too lost in the hell of her memories.

Just when she heard Matt's voice she was never sure, but it was so close that she opened her eyes in dismay, thinking that she was hallucinating.

Her heart lurched; he was climbing steadily towards her.

'Just stay still,' he called clearly. 'I'll be with you in a minute, and then we'll get you down.'

'No,' she whispered, her heart in her mouth. There wasn't enough room for another adult on the ledge. All fear for herself fled; she could only think that her stupid terrors had put him in danger, know with a conviction so stark it almost made her cry out that if her panic caused him to be hurt she would go grieving down to her grave.

Mute, her eyes enormous in her drawn face, she watched as he made his way up the cliff. Some detached part of her admired his confidence, the smooth power of his movements, graceful, controlled, but the woman who loved him was held rigid by fear.

And when at last he stopped, just below the ledge, she croaked, 'Oh, why did you come? You might fall.'

His teeth flashed in a reckless grin. 'Darling, I've been climbing this ever since I was five.'

Some of the sick horror had receded, but at his words it came flooding back. He was watching her closely; he suddenly called to the unseen watchers, 'Turn off the spotlights.'

Instantly they were alone in the sable and silver night. Very quietly, but imperatively, Matt commanded, 'Lora. Tell me.'

She drew a deep, sobbing breath. 'I thought I'd got over it.'

'Have you always been afraid of heights, or was there a precipitating factor that you can remember?'

Once she had thought that she would die before she spoke of it, but she found the words coming easily, even as her hands clenched a deathgrip on the ledge. 'My father was a pathologically jealous man. He hated the fact that my mother had been married before, and for years he made Sandy's life a living hell, because he was a reminder that another man had had her first.'

There was a muffled sound from the man below her, and she defended herself drearily, 'That's what he used to say. Over and over again. Things got worse when she had me. He thought—or pretended to think—she loved me more. When I was two we went for a holiday to Queenstown and they argued, I think, although I can never remember her arguing. Not after that, anyway. Whatever happened, he held me out over a cliff—I can't remember where it was, except that it seemed to be hundreds of feet down, and he threatened to drop me.'

His hand shifted, clamped down over hers. The fingers were strong and warm. He said something she was glad she couldn't quite hear.

She hurried on, 'I can remember my mother crying and pleading, and the absolute terror of swinging above hundreds of feet of nothing, with rocks below, but then I think I must have fainted, because that's all I remember. After that I was terrified of heights.'

'I'm not surprised. What happened? Did your mother leave him?'

She gave a cynical little laugh. 'No. He said he loved her, and to her, that excused everything: the beatings, the constant mental torment—after all, love rules the world, isn't that right? Love excuses everything—anything.'

He was silent for a long moment while she cursed herself for giving away so much, and then he said calmly, 'Then they both needed psychiatric treatment.'

'Need,' she said on a half-sob. 'They're still alive, still playing their games.'

Silence, as though that keen, clever brain was weighing everything she said. 'But you managed to overcome the fear. You can climb.'

'I wasn't going to be handicapped by it. I couldn't bear to think that something they had done was going to mark me for life. Not if I could do anything about it. So I got professional help. And Sandy was wonderful. He took me tramping and climbing—he was totally patient. I never learned to love it, but I became quite confident. Coming up, that is. I've never liked going back down.'

'I see.' Another long moment before he said, 'Well, if you're going to get off this cliff we'd better go.'

Instantly she panicked. She knew what he was doing, knew too that he was right, but she sat for long, miserable moments before saying fiercely, 'Matt, I'm so *frightened*.'

'I know.' He held her mesmerised in the still starlight by the compelling force of his will. 'You know you can do it. You would never have made it up here if you hadn't been a good climber. I think you may have regressed because Moana reminded you of yourself that first time, small and afraid and totally helpless, but you beat it once, and you can do it again. The ropes are already here. All you have to do is slide into the strop and do up the grommet. And keep your arms down by your sides! Use your feet to fend off the rock.'

When she hesitated, he said persuasively, 'I can't promise you that the rope won't break. The lesson you learned so cruelly, that you can only trust yourself in this world, is valid. But you trusted Moana to them. Can't you trust yourself?'

And when she said nothing he went on, 'Or is it me you don't trust? I checked those ropes——'

How to tell him that she would trust him with her life, that she was only afraid that if she fell she would take him with her?

In a voice barely audible above the water, she said, 'Will you go down first? I want you safe first.'

His teeth flashed in the starlight. 'Oh, Lora, haven't you worked out that if you fall I want to fall with you? Endangered—I was at risk the first time I saw you, and each subsequent day has made me fall deeper and deeper into the quicksand.' He laughed deeply at her astounded face. 'We'll go down together. You don't need the ropes. Come on, my love—do this for me.'

Just for a moment she froze again, but his astounding words gave her the courage to follow. Biting her lip in an intensity of fear, she swivelled around, face to the wall, and lowered herself over the edge.

His hand touched her ankle. 'A little to the right,' he instructed, 'six inches or so—yes, that's it. And swing your body to the left again—fine. You're doing well.'

It was slow, painfully slow, and exhausting, but with his voice encouraging her and his occasional light touch on her leg she managed to make it down, to collapse at the bottom in a torrent of tears in his arms.

'It's all right,' he said, holding her tightly. 'You did well, darling.'

Fortunately there were others there so she managed to stifle the weeping without making too much of a fool of herself; she certainly didn't pour out the love and gratitude which were roiling around in her, clouding her normally cool mind with their dangerous fumes.

And by the time she got back to the house she had regained control and was cursing herself for her stupidity. He was too astute not to have made the connections she had given away; he would understand only too well her fearful reluctance to commit herself, and no doubt he would see himself as the man who could help her overcome the conditioning of her childhood.

She was rigid with the effort not to give in to that weak part of her which yearned for love and desired only to lose itself in a man's love. Oh, she knew that Matt bore no resemblance to her father, but in a way he would demand more, and she was afraid that she was capable of only a limited love, too suspicious to be able to give him the unbounded, all-encompassing emotion he deserved.

But he made no attempt to follow up on their conversation—indeed, once back at the house he had no opportunity, for he went off into the night to keep vigil with Meri and Rod at the hospital, and after a cup of tea and a bath Lora took herself off to bed, pushing the

events of the afternoon to the back of her mind with a
savage single-mindedness which was helped by weariness.

But she knew that there would be a reckoning, and
soon. His eyes had told her that as they had blazed heated
amber into hers when he'd left.

CHAPTER NINE

IT TOOK Lora a long time to get to sleep, but when she awoke it was early, not far from dawn. She lay quietly in the bed watching the branches of the jacaranda silhouetted against the paler sky, and wondered what had woken her. A sound from outside the door brought her upright: Matt's voice, pitched very low as he said her name.

Instantly she ran across the room. He hadn't been to bed, for he wore the clothes he had had on the night before, and his face was a little more drawn than usual. He looked wonderful.

'How is she?' Lora asked breathlessly.

His face creased into a smile. 'She's fine. A slight concussion, that's all. When she woke she was rather grumpy because she hadn't found the horsey.'

'I wondered if that was where she had headed. But how was it that she wasn't seen before she got anywhere near the falls?'

He pushed a hand at the back of his neck, and stretched, the muscles in his shoulders and arms bulging beneath the thin material of his shirt. 'Sheer bad luck. She moved much faster than anyone thought she could, and by the time the alarm was given she was already half-way down the cliff-face, hidden by the trees and scrub. She must have heard them calling, but she knew she wasn't supposed to be there so I presume she lay low. I don't know how the hell she got out on to that ledge, but she was trapped when the second slip took more of the cliff away. She told Meri she fell over and banged her head. After that I think she must have dozed most of the time.'

'Thank heavens.' Lora shivered, remembering that narrow ledge.

He nodded, looking down at her with an enigmatic glint beneath his heavy eyelids. 'Meri and Rod want to see you to thank you some time tomorrow.'

She flushed, suddenly aware that she had on nothing but a fairly scantily cut nightshirt. His narrowed gaze made her conscious of the fact that her breasts thrust against the thin material, and her legs stretched long and sleek and warm beneath it.

'Thank you for telling me,' she said nervously, stepping back.

He yawned, then reached out and fingered a pale tress of hair that nestled into the vulnerable spot where her neck met her shoulder. 'Not the way I'd intended to spend the night,' he observed smoothly. 'But I'm too bushed to be any good to you now. Sleep well, because I'm not going to let you off that promise you made yesterday. Tomorrow night you'll be in my bed, and there won't be much rest for you there.'

She blushed and said, 'I—yes, all right. Goodnight.'

He laughed beneath his breath and put out a hand to pull her into him, holding her for a long moment against him. Exhausted though he had to be, she felt the stirring in his body, primeval appetite responding to the nearness of a receptive woman. A great wave of love mingled with the desire that his presence always caused, but beneath it, like black threads inextricably woven with the gold, pulsed a fierce, feral possessiveness.

She said, 'Matt—come to bed with me.'

He eased his hold, using his hand to push up her chin. His eyes were like topazes, glittering and hard, and he said, 'Your eyes are so clear, pale and clear as ice, I should be able to read every thought behind them. Yet I still have no idea how your mind works. No, I won't go to bed with you now. I'm no masochist, and I'm not going to take you for the first time with people hammering on the door and demanding to know where you are! Besides, I'm too tired to follow my baser instincts, which impel me to spend hours discovering exactly what pleases you until we both lose control and I can do what I've wanted to do since the first time I saw you: lose myself in your beautiful body.'

However cleverly phrased, it was a rejection, and it stung even while her body quickened into life; she managed to ignore the cold little stab at her heart. 'All right,' she said on a half-smile. 'I'll see you in the morning.'

Surprisingly, he hesitated, before bending to kiss her forehead. 'We'll work it out,' he said comfortingly.

What? The fact that she was as fatally flawed as her father? How could anyone work that out?

At least he wasn't offering marriage. Marriage was permanent, and if he had proposed she had a horrible feeling that she wouldn't have had the strength to say no.

She would never express her jealousy, never allow him to know that she could not bear to see him with another woman, she thought as a cockerel practised crowing in the warming light of day. He need never know that she was as dangerous as her father. She would love him with all of her being, and when it was over she would walk away with a smile and he would never know that it was tearing her heart out to go.

Her resolution was to be sorely tested. Matt was still asleep when Keren came into the office, slender and seductive in a jumpsuit that would, Lora decided after the first look, have done better with a shirt underneath the bib. But she had to admit that the smooth expanse of tanned shoulders rising from the white cotton was extremely inviting.

Lora gave her a civil greeting, waiting with no sign of impatience while Keren explained with wide, innocent eyes that she thought Matt would be up, and that she wanted to discuss something private with him.

Unfortunately he arrived half-way through this, still slightly rumpled-looking, his tawny hair not as smoothly combed as normal but his splendid vitality not at all depleted. And he did not appear to find Keren in the way, greeting her with his usual teasing charm before sweeping her out of the room without a backward glance.

It was Keren who delivered that, a triumphant slanting smirk that was a taunt. Lora felt a sick tide of anger and jealousy that increased to danger proportions when she heard Keren's gleeful chuckle.

She sat for long moments, fighting with every ounce of her will-power the insistent need to go out and intervene, to somehow drive Keren away with such finality that she would never come near Matt again, never dare to hang on his arm as though she had a right to.

After half an hour she heard the sound of an engine from the front of the house, and got to her feet and made her way out on to the veranda. Her face was set and pale, the bones sharp beneath the smooth veil of skin. She had to see Matt; she knew now that she could not bear to become his lover.

The anguish and cruel bitterness she had just endured had shown her how hopeless it was. Jealousy was a despicable emotion, but most people felt it. It was when it threatened to overcome all of her principles, all her standards, to engulf her in a shaming, degrading miasma, that she knew she had to run.

Better to leave him, to go back to the life she had made for herself; barren it might be, but at least she was safe from inflicting her pain on anyone else.

At the door out on to the veranda she stopped, acid burning through her veins. Keren, her body flowing and sinuous, had flung herself into Matt's arms and was kissing him with a vast enthusiasm which he seemed to be reciprocating. The sun gleamed like honey on his bent head; as he put her away from him Lora heard his low chuckle, amused and sensuous.

The pen in her hand cracked; emotionlessly she looked down at the mess the ink in the barrel was making in her palm, then turned and went back inside to wash it off.

He was in the office—without Keren—when she returned, leaning against the desk as he read through a report she had just finished typing. As she came in he lifted his head, fixing her with a long, cool stare. She knew that he had seen her watching them, and the colour came unbidden to her skin.

'I'm sorry,' she said, forcing the words out. 'I thought she had gone and I needed to know——'

He said gently, 'She was thanking me for using my influence with her uncle to let her go on a trip with some friends.'

Lora nodded, her heart cold and determined. 'She has a crush on you.'

'Yes. I know she's been a nuisance to you, but I refuse to believe that you ever thought there was any possibility of my falling in love with her.'

'You were just being kind to her,' Lora said with a painful, twisted smile.

He set the papers down and came towards her, stopping in astonishment as she backed away, her expression so tormented that it shocked him.

'No,' she said tiredly. 'It's no good, Matt. I can't go through with it.'

'Why?' The word was soft, without threat, yet she shivered and refused to meet his narrowed eyes.

'It wouldn't work out.'

There was a moment's taut silence before he said, 'I never thought you were a coward, Lora.'

If only he knew! Aloud she whispered, 'Well, I am. I can't——'

'You don't trust me not to abuse you?' His voice hardened. 'I can't *prove* that I won't be as jealous as your father, Lora, but why is it so difficult to believe that I'm not as twisted and unnatural as he is? Trust is vital in any relationship. You trusted me to get you down off that cliff last night.'

She couldn't bear him to think that she suspected him of such unbalanced behaviour. Although it was like flaying herself of her protective skin, she would have to tell him. Avoiding his frowning regard, she sank down into the office chair beside her computer console and said in a dull voice, 'Oh, Matt, it's not you! I trust you with my life! It's myself I can't trust. I'm just like my father.'

A thick silence pressed down; she could feel his eyes on her and dared not look up in case she saw—what? Contempt? No, she didn't fear that. Revulsion, the abhorrence of the normal for the unnatural. Matt was a possessive man, and his emotions, his reactions were strong, but they were not driven by morbid aberrations. She could not bear to see his desire replaced by repugnance.

But when he spoke, it was nothing like that. Astounded, she looked up, and saw that he was laughing.

'Dear heaven,' he said, when he could, 'I expected to have to spend months convincing you that I would never put you through the hell your mother sees as some sort of corollary to loving, but it never occurred to me that you might consider yourself tainted by your father's illness. Lora, look at me!'

She had averted her face; now, reluctantly, she turned to see him smiling tenderly down into hers. 'You have the clearest eyes,' he said gently, 'and the sweetest, sanest smile in all the world. How can you believe that you're not normal?'

Bitter pain wrenched at her heart. 'If I needed any convincing, it happened when I saw Keren kissing you,' she managed to say, her voice low and throbbing with shame. 'I could have killed her. I tell you, I *know* what it's like. I couldn't put anyone through that. Before very long you would find it impossible to cope with, and

I——' She hesitated, and changed her mind. 'I couldn't bear to drive you away.'

It was as near as she was likely to come to admitting that she had done the unforgivable and fallen in love with him. But he understood, for this time when he spoke his voice had altered, become reflective. 'Very well, then,' he said. 'If you really feel that, then you must go.'

Astonished, hurt unutterably because she had expected him to try to persuade her, she looked up. He was staring at her with a glittery, dangerous expression, his face set in lines of formidable control. All she could think of to say was, 'I'll leave today.'

He nodded, and waited until she had almost reached the door before saying indifferently, 'If you change your mind, you know where I live.'

Anguish hardened her voice. 'Oh, you'll soon find another woman to share your bed.'

'I'll still want you.'

How could he be so cruel? But even as she drove the long road back to Auckland she knew that he was not being cruel. She had allowed herself to indulge in wishful thinking, and had been punished only by herself for dreaming that she meant more to him than a convenient female body.

Auckland was the same. Hot, busy and impersonal, with everyone gearing up for Christmas, that cruellest of seasons when one was alone. Gavin had left the agency, gone no one seemed to know where, and she was soon too busy trying to bring some sort of order to the affairs of a woman who thought she had it in her to be a sharemarket tycoon to ponder his absence.

Not too busy, however, to miss Matt. In the slow, tiring weeks before Christmas, Lora learned the real meaning of despair, and bitter pain and cold, hard sexual frustration. In that dark time of her soul she had only one thought to cling to: that at least Matt would never experience the misery and humiliations she would have inflicted on herself if she had stayed as his lover.

Yet, out of all this came some good. For the first time
in her life she began to achieve some dim sort of comprehension of the torments her father suffered. Buried
deep beneath the bitter resentment was born a painful,
reluctant understanding. She could not bear to visit her
parents, but she rang them up on Christmas Eve, and
went to the midnight service afterwards with a calmer
mind than she had thought possible after dealing with
the suspicion and anger that was her father's usual reaction to any communication from her.

And then, on a most unseasonal Christmas morning
of wind and rain, Sandy arrived all the way from Canada
like a totally unexpected present, and with him the slim,
calm girl he was going to marry.

There were tears and laughter, the usual amount of
overeating and celebration, and in the afternoon, when
Lauren crashed with jet lag and too much food and excitement, Sandy and Lora sat down to talk. Outside the
wind was still howling around the block of units, the
rain spitting down. It wasn't cold, but it was a scene
ideal for confidences.

'You've changed,' Sandy said quietly.

He wouldn't ask why, of course. They were both
paranoid about privacy. Lora had to grit her teeth before
she could say, 'Sandy, why did you go to Canada? Was
it because you couldn't get a job here?'

He looked astonished. 'Is that what you thought? No.
After—after what I did to Matt Duncan, I was too
ashamed to stay.'

Shame clawed at her, but all that she said was a muttered, 'I see.' However, after a tense silence, she looked
across at him and said, 'I've just come back from
Kahurangi. I organised a field day for him.'

A little pale, he nodded, watching her closely. 'How
is he?'

'Fine.'

Another silence, then he said, 'I think you had better
tell me, love.'

'Stupidly, I fell in love with him.' Bald as the words were, it was a relief to get them out.

'And he?'

She shrugged. 'Oh, he was willing.'

Sandy sat up straight. 'Willing for what?'

Lora's full mouth quirked in a smile. 'Anything I was willing for,' she said calmly.

He relaxed, looking both annoyed and sheepish. 'Sometimes I forget you're a big girl. Do you want to tell me what went wrong?'

'I discovered that I'm like Dad.' There, she'd said it.

'Piffle,' Sandy said calmly.

Lora stared at him in astonishment. His pleasantly ugly face was serene and unmoved; he was smiling as though she had made a joke.

She faltered, then said on a drawn breath, 'Oh, I wish it was. But it's true. I was sick with jealousy, even when I *knew* there was no reason for it.'

He asked with placid confidence, 'Have you ever been in love before?'

'I—no.' She eyed him warily, loving the humorous quirk to his mouth, the dear, kind saneness of him. 'I'd never let myself get to that stage. I think I must have known...'

'Jealousy, especially when one is uncertain, is a normal part of falling in love.' Sandy leaned forward, stopping her from talking by touching her mouth with a fond forefinger. 'Lora, when I went to university I had a friend who was majoring in psychology, and he did a bit of research for me on that subject. It is an illness, and it can be traced back to childhood. That sort of aberration shows up early. You have never shown any signs of any pathological condition. You've never been possessive of me, or your friends; you welcomed Lauren today with real delight. You love honestly and deeply, but you are not afflicted with the lust to dominate or the fear of losing the object of your affections. You can trust others; the only person you don't trust is yourself.'

She said miserably, 'That's all very well, but I know how I feel.'

'You think you do.' Sandy looked at her downbent head with sympathy. 'What you're dealing with here is a whole new set of emotions, very strong ones. Most people have had crushes or love affairs by your age, but you've never allowed yourself to do that. Understandably, you've steered clear of any sort of emotional ties, seeing them as some sort of prison with no remittance for good behaviour. You have to learn to trust your instincts, Lora. Once you've done that, you'll see that you have nothing in common with your father.' He stopped, and went on, 'Just as you have nothing in common with Mum. You don't see her behaviour as a normal response to a normal attitude on her husband's part, do you?'

Lora was silent, turning his words over in her head. She wanted to believe him so much...

Finally she said on a sigh, 'No, of course not. But oh, if what you say is true, Matt was right and I must be the biggest coward on this earth.'

'I doubt it. You were afraid, and fighting a valiant rearguard action. How about a man who, because he'd made a mistake, couldn't even live in the same country as the man he'd wronged, but had to take himself and his painful conscience overseas?'

She said quietly, 'We allow ourselves to be ruled by other people, don't we?'

'We grew up afraid, you more than me, because I can dimly remember a saner life than the one your father thinks is normal. You should have known, though. If you were like him, you wouldn't have left Matt because you were afraid you might make him suffer. It's a sign of real, honest love when you give up your own happiness for someone else's. If you don't at least try to prove yourself wrong, you're letting your father rule your life as nakedly as though he's still standing over you. Is that what you want?'

She gave him a twisted smile. 'You know it's not.'

'Then give it a try.'

'And if you're wrong? If I am flawed?'

Sandy smiled at her. 'Get help,' he said calmly. 'You don't have to live with something like that. That's the mistake our parents made; neither of them will admit there's something wrong.'

With Sandy there, it all seemed so easy. But, when he and Lauren had left to stay with her parents in the South Island, Lora found her confidence sagging. Fresh to her mind came that last morning, when Matt had been so offhand, so uninterested in her final refusal. Almost as though he had believed that she was tainted by her father's illness.

As the city wound down the old year, tired and almost empty of people, she wrestled with her options, a war of heart and mind, at one moment hopeful, the next despairing.

She went to a New Year's party at an old friend's place and tried to forget her problems in the gaiety of the occasion, only to find herself avoiding the obligatory kisses at midnight because she felt unfaithful.

It was then that she decided that she was going to have to pull herself together. And she was going to have to do it soon, before she behaved like some dim-witted Victorian maiden and pined herself away into a decline. The agency, like most other New Zealand businesses, closed over the Christmas and New Year break, so she had another week before she was due back at work.

The first thing to do was go back to Kahurangi.

Matt might laugh at her, tell her it was too late. Well, she thought wearily, perhaps she deserved it. At least she would have tried.

She made her plans with her usual care. It would probably never be her temperament to be spontaneous, but Matt had wanted her as she was, deliberate, careful and cautious as hell. And if he no longer wanted her, then—there was a glory in having loved. Surely in time she would learn to love again, this time with openness and candour.

A month after she had left Kahurangi she came back to it, in the purple dusk of a summer evening. She was later than she had planned because the wretched car had had a puncture south of Whangarei and she had waited while the tyre was fixed, but she travelled with the evening star glowing like a great pearl in the west, and she took that as an omen of hope.

The bay was dusted with a confetti of yachts, and in the sky to the east the hills which guarded the entrance were gleaming ochre and gold and purple against a sea tinted with the rose of sunset.

Lora's heart swelled. For the first time in her life she felt the sensation of homecoming.

But she checked in at the motel she had reserved, and showered. It was just as well, for at Kahurangi Jane greeted her with a cool composure which chilled her to the bone.

'I'm afraid Matt is out,' she said, and looked significantly at the door.

The old Lora would have been so afraid of rejection that she would have shrivelled beneath her stiff façade, but the new one said calmly, 'I'll wait.'

Jane hesitated, but after a glance at Lora's face, capitulated. 'Very well, then, although I don't know when he'll be back.'

Lora allowed herself a wry smile. 'I have all the time in the world,' she said as she stepped inside.

Jane showed her to the sitting-room, the formal, beautiful heart of the homestead, then left her. There could be no doubt where her sympathies lay. Lora walked out to the terrace, leaning against the rail with a feeling that she had indeed burned her boats. But mingled with the apprehension and the fear was an excitement that brought a glitter to her eyes and a high colour to her cheeks. For if Matt still wanted her he would lose no time in taking her to bed, and now, all fears resolved, she would give herself to him with an ardour that had grown almost uncontrollably over the dark weeks of absence.

The colours of sunset faded, turned into the deep, dark blue and silver of night, and around the bay a slender necklace of golden lights sprang into prominence. The faint breeze from the sea died, to be replaced by an equally gentle breath from inland, warm and smelling of ripeness, of trees and hay and flowers. In spite of the many holidaymakers it was very quiet, very still. The turmoil of apprehension eased in Lora's heart, became almost peace.

Ignoring the slight dampness of the dew, she stayed out on the terrace. Towards nine o'clock Jane emerged and suggested that, as Matt seemed to have stayed out to dinner, perhaps she should leave a message and come back the next day.

'If I do that, I'm not likely to come back ever,' Lora admitted with a wry composure that didn't hide her determination.

The housekeeper's searching look flicked the surface of that composure. 'Perhaps that might be the best idea,' she said stiffly.

Lora nodded. 'Perhaps, but I'll let Matt be the judge.'

Strangely indecisive, Jane hovered, then said, 'Are you expecting to stay the night? Because——'

'No, I managed to get a room at one of the motels.'

Patent relief coloured the older woman's voice as she said, 'In that case I'll go off to bed. I have a headache.'

'I'm sorry,' Lora said, turning to her with a concerned look. 'Would it be better for you if I left?'

She was snatching at straws because something—a hint of warning, of pity?—in Jane's manner made her distinctly uneasy. And she was almost disappointed when Jane said hastily, 'No, I know you're not going to run away with the spoons!' She hesitated, before finishing flatly, 'It's none of my business, but I hope you haven't come to upset things again.'

'So do I,' Lora said with bleak emphasis.

Apparently satisfied, Jane nodded, said goodnight and departed, leaving her unwelcome visitor in a state of near panic.

It was a sensation which kept recurring until Lora was almost frozen with it, torn between the need to see Matt again and a fear that he had found someone else, that Jane had been trying to convey a warning.

When the lights flashed along the road between the great jacaranda trees she gave a strange little moan and had to cling for a moment to the railing before the steel in her spine brought her upright, her shoulders rigidly held straight, all expression wiped from the smooth contours of her face. She ran her fingers through her hair, lifting the mass of it away from her neck, conscious of the dampness of the strands at her temple. Her hand was cold, and trembled.

It seemed an eternity before the garage door thunked shut, another age until she heard laughter and a woman's voice, and knew then that Jane had been trying to warn her as much as her loyalty to Matt would allow her.

Nausea roiled in her stomach. She swayed under a betrayal so severe that it seemed like a blow to the heart. Then she lifted her head with a cold pride. She would fight . . . she had become a fighter.

She did not look towards the house, so the sound of Matt's voice, empty of all emotion, whipped a startled cry from her lips. He said her name again, and she heard that same woman's voice from inside, calling him.

'I'm sorry,' she said at last into the unfriendly air, 'I didn't realise that—I didn't know. I'll go.'

'My cousin and her husband are here.' He spoke absently, as though his former mistress meant nothing to him. As Lora drew an astonished breath he went on, 'Why are you?'

'You told me that when I had learned to trust myself I could come back.'

She hadn't looked at him, not once. Too afraid that she might see rejection. But now she turned her head.

The handsome leonine head was held as high, the striking good looks of the man blazed forth with eye-catching starkness, the line of mouth was every bit as determined. Yet he looked tired, his magnificent male vitality dimmed.

Lora said huskily into the fragrant air, 'If I'm too late, I'll go.'

'What changed your mind?'

She winced, but he deserved his pound of flesh. 'I've discovered what life is like without you. I've been functioning, but I wouldn't say I was alive.'

'I've always known that you want me.' His voice was even, almost reflective, yet she sensed his whole attention bent on her, the keen lance of his gaze trying to penetrate the fleshy covering of her body to see into the brain beneath. Matt would never be satisfied with smooth outward forms; he wanted the truth. That was why she had fled from him. She had spent all of her life in hiding, and the thought of opening up, allowing him access to her innermost being, was as frightening as anything she had ever encountered before.

The wind roved across her skin and she shivered.

'Wanting is common coinage,' he said. 'Is that what brought you back, Lora? Think carefully, because if I take you I'm going to take everything. I can't change my character, and I am a possessive man. You'll belong to me, completely and forever. I'll expect your absolute trust and your absolute faith. Can you cope with that?'

CHAPTER TEN

'YES,' Lora whispered, mesmerised by the stark purpose in the deep tones.

Matt held out his hand. She walked across to him and put her cold fingers into it; he enclosed them in a grip as sure and as warm as summer.

She said suddenly, 'But I think I must have *some* of my father in me, because I'm possessive, too. Can you cope with that?'

Amusement was a lion's purr in the back of his throat. 'Oh, I think so. I think so, my darling.'

From inside the house a woman laughed. Matt turned his head and said with great enjoyment. 'Come and meet Amber and Alex. They are the only close family I have.'

She didn't want to, she wanted nothing more than to feel the solace and reassurance of his arms again, but the doorway was blocked by a tall figure as a slightly accented voice said chidingly, 'What are you doing out there, my friend? Communing with nature?'

'A force of nature, certainly,' Matt returned coolly, drawing Lora with him to the door.

Amber and Alex Stephanides were the most stunning couple Lora had ever seen, their superb good looks enhanced by the sheen of extreme wealth and excellent taste. Lora had never considered herself to be shy, but when Matt introduced her without any comment she felt unwonted colour burn her cheeks at the quickly hidden speculation in both sets of eyes.

A lift of her head brought it erect; something in Alex Stephanides' dark eyes softened, and he smiled at her with all of his considerable charm. 'I am sorry we kept you waiting, Miss Reynolds. I hope it was not too long.'

Apparently she had passed some test. Not, however, one devised by Amber, who was watching with a hint of reserve. Her smile, however, was perfectly friendly as she shook hands. Lora felt an enormous let-down. How on earth could she hope that Matt might love her when, compared to Amber Stephanides' radiance, she was so very ordinary-looking?

Her eyes flew to Matt's face, but she could read nothing there but bland interest, and she knew that he was going to make her go through this with no help.

'No, I've been soaking in the peace,' she said lightly.

Amber nodded, but that intentness remained in her scrutiny. 'It is lovely, isn't it? I'm always happy to come back to Kahurangi. Where do you live, Miss Reynolds?'

'Auckland,' she replied, a spark of anger lighting up the pale depths of her eyes. She turned her head to look Matt in the face and finished calmly, 'But I'll be living here when Matt gets around to marrying me.'

There was an appalled silence. Perhaps the most shocked of them all was Lora herself, but she held her head high and ignored the colour that was scorching her skin, as she waited for Matt to answer her challenge.

To her astonishment he threw his head back and laughed, and when he had regained control took her hand and drew her close. 'When?'

'In three days,' she said promptly.

'Done.' And he bent his head and kissed her, hard and fast.

Shameless desire held Lora still. Until Amber said, 'You can't possibly get married in three days' time, Matt!'

Lora began to tremble, the bubble of delight folding, wilting, collapsing around her. She heard Alex ask shortly, 'Why?' and waited with painful tension for the answer.

'Because Lora won't have a dress! And how on earth can we organise a proper reception in three days? Poor Jane will have a fit.'

Alex laughed and said something, the words lost as Matt said calmly and positively, 'In that case, we'll have to elope.'

'You can't possibly elope, no one would ever forgive you.' Amber sighed theatrically. 'I suppose we'll just have to do the best we can. Well, what are we waiting for? Why aren't we drinking champagne?'

Lora looked at her for the first time since her objection, and saw only amusement and laughter in her expression; the slackening of tension brought her slow smile, and to its normal radiance was added a new glory so that the Stephanideses blinked and looked at each other as though at last they understood.

It was over. The beautiful white dress had been lovingly hung in the wardrobe by a laughing Amber, the new blue dress donned. Lora was exhausted, but her eyes glowed and there was a lovely wild rose colour in her cheeks.

'You look like a Valkyrie,' Amber sighed from her position at the end of the bed.

'All plaits and bust?'

'Tall and graceful and elegant. You look stunning, as you must know.'

Surveying her, so small and flagrantly beautiful, Lora said tightly, 'I'd like to be little and delicate, so that men feel protective about me.'

The other woman looked startled, but her eyes were very clear as she stood on tiptoe and kissed Lora's cheek. 'Something is wrong in a culture where no woman is happy with her appearance. All you have to remember is that Matt loves you and that you are now his wife,' she said very firmly. 'And you had better make him happy, or you'll have me to answer to!'

Lora couldn't repress the pang of jealousy which tore through her, but she had seen enough of the Stephanideses in the last three days to know that they loved each other with a devotion which was rare and strong. Whether Amber had ever been Matt's mistress or not, her heart and soul belonged now to her husband, and she treated Matt with the affection of the cousin she called herself.

So she smiled at Amber, and said lightly, 'I'm absolutely terrified.'

'So you should be. I may be small, but I'm fierce.' The laughter faded and she said soberly, 'I hope you'll be very happy. Matt deserves the best, and I rather think he's got it. Now, let's go before he comes looking for you.'

Lora's mouth twisted in a wry, unseen smile. Matt had shown little enthusiasm for her company in the preceding days, but of course she couldn't say that.

However, as soon as she and Amber appeared in the doorway of the sitting-room he looked across, and for a moment the lazy gold of his regard heated to fire. It lasted only as long as it took for him to regain control, but that moment's betrayal comforted Lora as nothing else could have. Whatever he felt about her, whether he loved her or not, he wanted her.

If that was all there was, it would have to be enough.

They left from the bay in Matt's cruiser, and took the passage past Tapeka Point to the outer islands. Lora stood beside Matt, trying not to watch the muscles move in his arms as he guided the vessel across the water. She kept dragging her eyes away to look about at the magnificence of sea and islands, but they persisted in drifting back, and she was assailed by images of those dark lean fingers on her body, the barbaric impact of dark skin against the pale sleekness of hers.

She wondered whether to tell him that she bruised easily, then made a small, unseen grimace, chiding herself for being so melodramatic. This was no monster, this was Matt, whom she loved, with whom she was going to spend the rest of her life. What she was suffering from was the well-known virgin's nerves, combined with the equally famous bridal jitters.

The island, lent to them by Alex and Amber, was small and secret, the only one left in all the Bay of Islands with the forest cover still intact. The dark cloak of bush gave it a hidden, mysterious air, as though it had lain untouched since the beginning of all time. Matt brought the boat in through a shallow reef with care, cutting the engine so that they glided in to a wharf.

He looked down at Lora's composed face with an ironic smile. 'We're here.'

Here was a small house with sparsely furnished rooms opening out on to a wide terrace that overlooked the bay, and beyond it the wilder reaches of the mainland. The house was pretty and convenient, and easy to look after. It did not look like the sort of place a billionaire would choose to spend many of his holidays in. Lora said so, and was answered by that same ironic smile.

'Alex is Greek,' he said, as though that explained it.

'And that makes a difference?'

His shoulders moved in a shrug, as though he was tired. 'They tend to have simple tastes, and he's no exception. Would you like a shower?'

'I had one before we left.'

'Then let's go for a swim. Unless you'd like to do something else? Rest, perhaps?'

'No,' she said carefully, while her heart broke into several pieces. 'A swim would be lovely.'

'Get changed, then, while I turn on the power and the water.'

She put on a bikini, preferring its scanty covering to the high-cut legs of the latest one-piece fashions; her legs, she had thought when she bought it, were long enough without needing to show her hipbones, too. Firmly banishing a mocking image of Amber's slender fragility, she went out, bracing herself for Matt's gaze. He was nowhere to be seen, although she could hear him moving about in the rooms beneath the house. It was ridiculous to be so shy.

But she couldn't wait for him. As his footsteps started up an internal staircase she panicked and almost ran down the path to the beach, and by the time he followed her she was already in the sheltering water, swimming as if her life depended on it to the raft moored in the deep water.

The water was almost lukewarm, smooth as silk gliding across her limbs. She felt a sudden surge of the sensuality that she had spent so much of her life repressing, and with a recklessness she had never felt before she thought, why not?

Surely on her honeymoon a woman had the right to let herself go?

She pulled herself out of the water and lay on her back on the raft, limbs sprawled in relaxed looseness, her eyes closed against the power of the sun. After a moment she felt the raft dip as Matt lifted himself on to it. Slowly she raised her eyelids by the merest fraction. The sun caught the tiny drops of water tangled in her lashes, working a magic so that Matt stood surrounded by rainbows, the powerful, muscular lines of his body iridescent and glowing with colour.

A strange sensation drove the breath from Lora's lungs. She felt awe, as though she was a woman of old chosen for a god's pleasure, and a fervent primitive need, a force that came from deep, deep within her, that had been hidden in her cells waiting for this time, this man, this place.

Without volition, she reached out a hand. He dropped to the raft and took it, holding the palm to his mouth before he guided it to his chest. His skin was rough with hair, wet and yet hot, and beneath her sensitive finger-tips she felt the thunder of his heart.

'Lora,' he said very softly, very imperatively. 'Look at me. Open your eyes.'

She shook her head and he said again, 'Look at me so that you know who you belong to.'

At that, her lashes flew up and he laughed softly, sardonically. 'Yes, you don't like that, do you?'

'It sounds—chauvinistic,' she retorted.

His brows rose. 'It is. Uncivilised, too. What's been bred into mankind for who knows how many centuries is not banished in a generation. What could be more basic, more fundamental than a man and a woman, water and sunlight and this?'

His hand moved quickly, tracing with the possessiveness of a possessive man the soft curves of her breasts to the narrow indentation of her waist, the bowl of her hips, sleek and defined by a glaze of water, and all the time his eyes, burning now with a fire he made no attempt to hide, seared into hers in arrogant authority.

Lora's mouth dried. She knew what he was doing but she didn't know why; surely her return had been surrender enough to satisfy the alpha streak in him, the need to dominate?

She said his name and some of her fear must have shown in her face, for he said savagely, 'Yes, so you should be afraid. Do you have any idea how much I want you? Have wanted you from the time I first saw you? I thought you were a dream dragged up from my subconscious, because no one like you could exist.'

Colour burned through her skin and he smiled, the set smile of a man under pressure, and said gently, 'Oh, yes, I've wanted you enough to eat at my heart and my brain and my guts. For a while I thought I was not quite a man because I needed you so much. It's the first time I've lost my independence, you see. If I'd been able to see the joke I might even have found it amusing that when it happened, when I finally fell, it was for a woman who so obviously wasn't going to allow herself to fall in love with me.'

His hand moved to cup her breast, the long fingers loose yet not relaxed, as though he waited for her to try to get away. Needles of pure sensation, sharp as pain, sweet as ecstasy, ran through her body, rousing every cell to vivid, potent, singing life.

'The hardest thing I've ever done was let you go,' he said, still watching her face while his fingers worked their magic on her skin.

Her eyes widened. 'You seemed so—offhand.'

His mouth twisted in a self-derisory smile. 'You were under enough pressure. I had to let you go. It was the one thing I couldn't fight, yet I felt as though some part of me was bleeding to death when I had to stay and watch you walk away from me.'

'But when I came back you were so aloof. If you hadn't been so—so cold I wouldn't have got angry and forced the issue. You made me so angry I lost my temper, but I honestly didn't come back intending to pressure you into marrying me. I'd have been happy with what you wanted.'

'You didn't want anything I didn't want,' he said coolly. 'I had every intention of dragging you to the altar, whether you were ready for it or not. I was going to give you two months to work out that your supposedly uncontrollable jealousy was only a front you were hiding behind. What you were afraid of was giving yourself to me.'

He was, of course, right. Piqued at the way he could see right into her innermost heart and mind, she said pertly, 'You haven't shown any signs of wanting me. Very circumspect, you've been, since I dared you to marry me.'

'I wanted to show you that I could control myself.' He laughed into her astounded face. 'And to whet your appetite, of course.' He bent, but she held him off, her expression serious.

'Will you be able to forget what Sandy did? He has learned his lesson.'

'Of course I will. Every man is entitled to one mistake. I don't carry grudges.'

'If that's so, why did you think I'd come to cheat you? The night we saved the whales, you made it perfectly clear that you tarred me with the same brush,' she recalled sadly.

His hand moved to encircle her throat. The long fingers exerted slight pressure, then he bent his head and kissed the length of it. 'I was hitting back. If you hadn't said that I'd hounded him out of the country I'd never have thought such a thing.'

'I was stupid to think that,' she acknowledged. 'I know Sandy. He is proud——'

'As proud as you,' he interpolated smoothly.

'—and I should have realised that breaking trust like that was more than he could bear. He told me he had had to leave New Zealand, he couldn't work here any more, and I assumed it was because you were vindictively making it impossible for him to get another job. Instead, it was his own pride which was making it impossible.'

'And I,' he said, his mouth moving against her skin in the lightest of kisses, 'I was just as arrogant. I was furious because you could think such a thing of me, but I hid my hurt feelings by pretending to myself—and to you—that I had been fooled by a deceitful bitch whose only loyalty lay with her brother.'

'Did you really think that I'd inveigled my way into the job to seduce you into giving up this imaginary vendetta you were conducting against Sandy?'

The sun beat down on her face; his was buried in her throat, his wide shoulders blocking her from the sky and the wind. The moisture on their bodies had almost dried, but she was acutely conscious of the two thin layers of cloth that were all that separated them. Still wet, they might as well not have been there.

Her body was stirring, summoned by tides as old as time, as imperious. And against her, in an exciting, unhidden answer, she could feel the involuntary response of his.

'I didn't know,' he said slowly, lifting his head to look down at her. 'It seemed likely. You're a loyal sister. And apart from one or two occasions, which clearly you regretted, it was impossible to know how you felt about me.'

'But you were suspicious of me as soon as you saw me.'

'Afraid,' he corrected. He looked down at her sleek body, at the full mounds of her breasts, tipped now with small, sharp peaks straining against the cloth of her bikini, and he said urgently, 'I must have known right from the start that whatever I felt for you was not going to be the simple emotions I'd always thought were love. For years I thought I loved Amber, but it was nothing like the complicated sensations I felt for you. Desire, and liking—yes, I knew those, and a protective instinct, I'd felt all that with Amber, but with you it was something much more, something totally primal and wild, a kind of basic recognition. I'd spent all these years waiting for you, but when at last you came to me there was all this damned frustration stopping me from reaching out and claiming you.'

His mouth crushed any answer from hers, forcing it open to receive him in a famished kiss that stole all possibility of thought from her.

'Lora,' he groaned, 'oh, Lora, say that you love me, that it's not just one-sided. I need you so much—I've starved for you so long...'

Her heart was beating high and panic-stricken in her throat, but she managed to whisper, 'Of course I love you. How could I stop myself? You are all that I want in a man—I saw you and I fell all the way, mountains and seas and planetsful—why on earth do you think I came back?'

He dragged in a deep breath and lifted himself to his feet, pulling her with him in a movement which corded the muscles in his arm.

Once she was on her feet he looked very deep into her eyes. 'I don't know,' he said. 'Sex has to be about one of the most powerful instincts in the lexicon.'

Lora realised that he really wasn't sure of her. Her masterful, dominating Matt, so arrogant beneath the lazy veneer, didn't understand that she would follow him barefoot and naked across a continent of flint and fire.

She reached up to smooth the frown lines between his brows. 'I love you with all my heart, and all my soul, and all my body,' she said softly, the words a vow and a promise. 'I didn't realise that you loved me. I thought you were still in love with Amber, and that you had decided that I would be a good enough substitute, but I came back because life without you was like starving. I thought I'd give her damned ghost a run for its money.'

He laughed, the mocking teasing glint flickering, growing. 'Yes, that sounds like you.' The amusement died. 'And then when you came back she was there.'

She was still not sure enough of him to do any more than nod. He turned away, stepping back a little, leaving her bereft. After a still moment when she heard the forlorn piping of dotteral somewhere along the beach, he said abruptly, 'She was so beautiful, so young when she came here, and so sad, I suppose she brought out all my protective instincts. And over the years it became comfortable for me to think I loved her. But she has always loved Alex. When he found her and took her back to Greece I was happy for her. Oh, I missed her, as I'd miss a younger sister. But one look at you and I knew that all my previous notions about love had to be scrapped. This was a whole new ball game. I understood why Amber never saw me as a lover, never even saw me as a man. We never slept together.' He looked intently into her eyes. 'But you must have realised that when you saw them there. Alex loves her this side of idolatry, but he wouldn't bring her back to see me if we'd ever been lovers.'

Lora moved uncomfortably. 'I thought—well, you read such things about people... I thought perhaps you had a sophisticated outlook...'

He gave a sardonic snort of laughter. 'Alex is as jealous as hell, possessive to his fingertips. And I've discovered over these past months that I am every bit as primitive. Believe me, if I had ever loved Amber he would make sure that she stayed across the other side of the world, and if you think that I have a modern outlook on unfaithfulness, let me disabuse you of the idea right now.'

He was speaking with all of the passion of a very passionate man. Lora looked wonderingly at him, saw him take another deep breath and say through his teeth, 'I'm sick of talking. I seem to have spent years of my life waiting for this moment. I thought I'd be a perfect, modern, thoughtful man and let you rest and relax before we made love, but I'm afraid I want you too much. I'm afraid that I'll frighten you...'

Something hot and uncontrollable sprang into full-blown life in Lora, coursing through her in a flood of fire. With no more answer than a provocative smile over her shoulder she dived off the raft and into the water, heading for the shore.

He caught her up long before she reached it, but was content to swim alongside her until the tiny waves began to build. Then he stopped her by hauling her into his arms and holding her in an embrace which took her breath away. His lashes half hid the burning fire of his eyes. Without kissing her, he said harshly, 'I am not like your father, Lora. I am possessive, that's bred into me, and I will probably be jealous, possibly even unreasonably so, but I swear that I have no signs of the sickness that ruined your childhood.'

'I know that,' she sighed, her voice deep and deliberate. 'I wouldn't have come back if I'd thought otherwise. He is sick, and I think my mother must be too to accept his sickness. You are healthy, more sane than any man I've ever know. Clean and good...' Her voice died away. It was impossible to tell him how she thought of him. She said in a soft voice, 'Like water in the desert. I thought I'd never be able to respond to a man, never love without fear and suspicion and mistrust... Then I found you, but I was afraid, because although my life had been barren, I had been in control of it. But when I met you my heart suddenly took over and I didn't know what to do.'

'Are you still afraid?'

She smiled. 'No.'

Beneath her breasts she felt his heart pick up speed, the heavy, urgent thudding a counterpoint to the thick excitement of hers. 'That smile,' he said deep in his throat. 'You don't know what you do to me when you smile. Lora, I love you.'

So simple, those words, yet they contained all of heaven for her. And when his mouth came down she gave herself up entirely to the desire burning so fiercely because it had been held under such strict control.

'Lora.' Just one word, and then he was lifting her, carrying her up from the water and across the burning sand to the place where they had shed their towels. Still with her locked in his arms he sank to his knees, lowering her gently. Excitement throbbed in a primitive rhythm in her body, blocking out all thought but the sound of his name, her name on his lips.

She held out her arms and pulled him down, but he resisted. 'Not yet,' he said harshly. 'It will be better for you if we go up to the house.'

But the sun shone brilliantly on her shaking head. 'No,' she said firmly. 'Here, Matt.' And when he hesitated she ran a shy hand over the broad expanse of his chest, tugging gently at the almost dry hair. 'Please, darling.'

He smiled, and she knew she had won. His hand came up to clasp hers, holding it against him as if it were a talisman, a charm against his chest. The other hand moved to untie the string of her bikini top. She couldn't prevent the flinch, and immediately his hand stopped.

Sudden tears sprang to her eyes. In a shaking voice she said, 'I'm sorry, I'm sorry, I can't help it. I want you so much and I don't know what's going to happen and I'm very nervous, but I love you, Matt, I love you so much——'

'Wait a minute,' he said in an arrested voice. His hand left the bikini and caught her chin so that he could see into the torment in her expression. Speaking slowly, he said, 'Are you a virgin, Lora?'

She nodded, holding the words back behind the tight line of her lips.

His breath came out in a sudden exhalation, as though someone had hit him in the solar plexus. 'I thought— you said that you had never been able to respond to a man, and I though you had tried,' he said slowly.

The golden flames were reined in by that formidable will. He asked softly, 'Lora, my heart's delight, just how much experience in making love have you?'

And suddenly she saw that it was going to be all right. He was looking at her with a wry humour that was only a covering over a vast delight. 'Very little,' she confessed, blushing like a girl on her very first date.

He looked down at the voluptuous curves and ran a finger across the top of her breast. 'So this is new?'

'Ah—yes.'

His mouth followed the line his finger had taken. 'And this?' he said, the words an erotic little caress against her too sensitive skin.

'I—Matt!'

His mouth closed around the nipple, suckling warmly. 'This is not,' he said with great satisfaction. 'But now I know why you reacted so swiftly.'

'I've never been so excited in my life.'

The admission brought his head up. 'My dearest, that is only the beginning!'

It was. The little exchange had cleared the air, rid Lora of the fear that had been hampering her, the fear that he might be repelled by her gaucheness. He made love to her with all of his considerable skill, a long, loving wooing which whiled away the hours into dusk.

Lora had thought that nothing could be more exciting than his hands on her body, but she found that she was wrong. Matt showed her all of the ways for a man to pleasure his love, with his hands, with his mouth, with soft, husky words, at times as easy as the flow of the waves, at others impeded and urgent with hungers and needs neither of them had to fear expressing.

Lora discovered that her body could reach a pinnacle of ecstasy, and then, incredibly, that there were heights beyond heights, magnificent, soaring realms of rapture, mind and body so tense with pleasure that she moaned and whimpered with it, aching for a miraculous release which he withheld, although she could see the ferocious restraint he needed to use.

But at last, when she was sobbing with need, he said between his teeth, 'Lora—I must——'

She opened her eyes, beautiful eyes in which there was nothing but a passionate trust, and offered him the gift of her body, the rest of her life, all that she was and would be.

The evening sun gilded him, her golden man, body poised over her, his strongly marked features drawn with unendurable need. Not a flicker of fear showed in her face; she smiled, the blind, primeval smile of a woman for only one man in her life, and welcomed the joining, the slow entry into union, and the final involuntary thrust that joined them.

She cried his name, and he froze, demanding, 'My heart, did I hurt you?'

'No, oh, no. It feels—I don't know—Matt, it feels right...'

His mouth bent to hers, gently, mercilessly taking what he wanted. A fever beat through her, needing more than that kiss, more than the still pressure of his weight. She moved her hips, and as if it had been a signal he groaned and completed the stroke, making himself master of all that had been surrendered so willingly.

She saw the moment when his control snapped, fed on the splintering shards of his restraint as his head was flung back and the golden tide engulfing him caught her up and spun her around in a flood of sensation, whirling her beyond time and space for a few perilous moments.

Afterwards, when she was able to hear his voice above the thunder of her heart, she said weakly, 'Thank you.'

He was lying beside her, holding her against him. His chest rose as he said, 'Why? For the most shattering experience of my life? I should thank you.'

She said shyly, 'It can't be the same for you, though.'

'Because I wasn't a virgin?' He laughed and kissed the top of her head. 'I'm not as experienced as gossip makes out. For years I thought I was in love with Amber, and in a strange way I was faithful to her. And although I indulged in the usual amatory adventures in my randy youth, I suppose I always knew that there would be Lora waiting for me.' She could hear the amusement in his voice. 'I have been called cold.'

'Whereas you are really fastidious,' she said aggressively.

'That fierce loyalty!' He used his strength to lift her away from him so that he could see her face, lax and peaceful as it had never been before, the pale eyes soft and dreamy, the tender mouth slightly swollen and red. He said softly, 'I dreamed of a woman who was warm and soft and loving, and I got a Viking woman, tall and fierce and cold, with fires deep inside and a loyalty strong enough to break hearts on.'

She laughed, enjoying the way her breasts touched him, the way his eyes held hers so steadily, yet with a flame burning deep inside them.

'So you made love to her, and you got your warm, soft woman,' she said, settling sensuously down on his chest. With a catlike movement of her head, she bent to kiss his throat. 'Lucky Matt.'

He held her close, close, so that she could feel the stirring in his body, the pulsing tide of life through it. Her question darkened her eyes.

'Yes,' he said, immensely pleased as he got to his feet and pulled her up with him. 'At this moment I doubt whether any other man on this earth feels as lucky as I. Now, let's get up to the house. I want to feel what it's like to make love to you on a bed.'

It was wonderful, and afterwards she discovered that she was weeping a little, the tears blurring his concerned face. 'I can't bear it if it's going to keep getting better,' she said. 'I'll go mad.'

'Both of us,' he said, his breathing still too rapid. 'Or I'll die of a heart attack.'

'Why don't we just settle down into humdrum domesticity?'

'An excellent idea. Only I don't think it's going to happen. We have, however, sixty or so years to work on it.'

'Sixty years,' she said dreamily, the tears drying. She knew what he was trying to say. It would not always be like this, all fire and fury, but the love would always be there.

Harlequin Presents®

Coming Next Month

Take 4 bestselling love stories FREE

Plus get a FREE surprise gift!

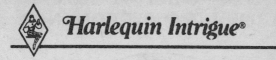
Harlequin Intrigue®

A SPAULDING & DARIEN MYSTERY
by Robin Francis

An engaging pair of amateur sleuths—Jenny Spaulding and Peter Darien—were introduced to Harlequin Intrigue readers in #147, BUTTON, BUTTON (Oct. 1990). Jenny and Peter will return for further spine-chilling romantic adventures in April 1991 in #159, DOUBLE DARE in which they solve their next puzzling mystery. Two other books featuring Jenny and Peter will follow in the A SPAULDING AND DARIEN MYSTERY series.